THE DEVIL'S ANVIL

Two kill-crazy McClory cousins have busted out of Yuma Pen, heading for Indian Territory. Somebody has to bring them in — and the job falls to Deputy US Marshal Liberty Mercer, who sets off to run the outlaws to ground. But to reach the McClory stronghold in Silver Rock Canyon, Mercer and her makeshift posse — Raven Bjorkman, her old friend; Latham Rawlins, brother of Liberty's one-time love Latigo; and the crooked Dunn brothers — must cross the deadly, searing desert known as the Devil's Anvil . . .

STEVE HAYES

THE DEVIL'S ANVIL

Complete and Unabridged

LINFORD
Leicester

First published in Great Britain in 2014 by
Robert Hale Limited
London

First Linford Edition
published 2016
by arrangement with
Robert Hale Limited
London

A catalogue record for this book is available
from the British Library.

ISBN 978–1–4448–2788–0

Published by
F. A. Thorpe (Publishing)
Anstey, Leicestershire

Set by Words & Graphics Ltd.
Anstey, Leicestershire
Printed and bound in Great Britain by
T. J. International Ltd., Padstow, Cornwall

This book is printed on acid-free paper

For
Chris and Georgie
With Love

1

Deputy US Marshal Liberty Mercer was sitting in the Hotel Guthrie dining room about to enjoy a wedge of hot apple pie when she saw Cyrus Lyman, the telegraph operator, appear in the doorway. Red-faced and out of breath, he was clutching a telegram, and though there were other customers around her eating lunch and she wasn't expecting any messages, she sensed he was looking for her and her stomach knotted.

Her gut feeling was seldom wrong. Today was no exception.

As soon as Lyman saw her, he headed straight for her table, his tight-lipped expression filled with concern. 'This j-just c-came in,' he panted, handing her the wire. 'It's urgent.'

'So I gathered,' she said dryly, 'else you wouldn't have run all the way over here, would you? Here.' She poured him a glass of water and indicated the chair across the table from her. 'Drink this and sit down before you fall down, Cyrus.'

He sat, grateful to regain his breath, gulped down the water and then mopped his forehead with the napkin lying before him.

Liberty opened the telegram and read it.

MCCLORY COUSINS ROY AND TRAVIS ESCAPED FROM YUMA TERRITORIAL PRISON STOP KILLED FOUR GUARDS STOP HEADED FOR INDIAN TERRITORY STOP BRING IN DEAD OR ALIVE STOP USE EXTREME CAUTION STOP BOTH MEN VOW NEVER TO BE CAPTURED ALIVE

US MARSHAL LANK C. RIVERS

Tucson, 4 October 1892

Liberty looked up from the telegram and gave a resigned sigh. A few weeks ago the McClorys had been captured following a month-long killing spree that had shocked even the most hardened lawmen. For no apparent reason other than sadistic pleasure the two outlaws had crisscrossed Arizona, killing men, women and children and then drunkenly bragged about it in saloons throughout the territory.

It was their bragging and rowdiness that eventually had gotten them captured by one of Marshal Rivers' deputies who'd entered the Wagon Yoke Saloon in Tucson as the cousins were shooting it up. He hadn't recognized them from their Wanted posters, and thinking they were just two drunken cowboys had pistol-whipped them from behind and dragged them off to jail. There, behind bars, Travis McClory had luridly described how he'd shot two young boys who'd caught him raping their mother. The deputy, upon realizing who his prisoners were, immediately wired the marshal and within hours the entire territory knew of the McClorys' capture.

Their trial was brief. Both men were

found guilty of murder by Judge Isaac Parker and taken to Yuma Territorial Prison to await their death by hanging.

Liberty had read about the McClorys' trail of blood in the *Guthrie Daily Leader* during the trial; and now, knowing the danger she was facing and the days, maybe weeks in the saddle that lay ahead, wondered if she'd made a mistake by becoming a lawman.

But only for a moment.

Then her sense of duty kicked in and it never entered her head to ignore the telegram or find an excuse as to why she couldn't go after the McClorys; especially knowing who'd sent it. Marshal Lank Rivers was a legend throughout the southwest. Her boss, Marshal Canada Thompson, respected him as much as he respected her friend and mentor, Marshal Ezra Macahan, in El Paso — high praise indeed.

Liberty absently ran her fingers through her short tawny hair, then read the telegram again and told Lyman: 'Wire Marshal Rivers back saying that I received this and will act accordingly.'

'What about Marshal Thompson?'

'I'm sure he's already received the same wire.'

'He has. But — '

'What then?'

'Shouldn't I notify Rivers that the marshal's tied up in Tulsa?'

'For what purpose?'

'Well, I . . . uh . . . just thought — '

' — Marshal Rivers should know that the lawman he's relying upon to capture two of the territory's deadliest outlaws is a — woman?'

'N-No, that ain't it all.'

'That's exactly it, you miserable old hypocrite,' Liberty said, flaring. 'My God, Cyrus, what do I have to do to convince you and the other men in Oklahoma that I'm capable of doing my job?'

Lyman shifted uneasily and refused to meet her angry brown-eyed stare. Shy by nature, he'd always felt intimidated by this tall, lithe, vibrant young woman who, despite being schooled by nuns at St Marks, a convent in Las Cruces, New Mexico, had possessed the skill and fortitude to become a law officer.

'I mean, how long must I be a deputy marshal before folks here start accepting and trusting me?' she demanded.

Lyman shrugged and continued to look everywhere but at Liberty.

'I've done everything anyone's expected of me, haven't I? Well, *haven't I?*' she repeated when he didn't answer.

'S-Sure.'

'Then dammit, give me a chance to earn my spurs and stop questioning my grit!'

Lyman looked hurt. 'I was just askin' you a question, deputy. No need to throw a shoe.'

'Get out of here, you old goat,' Liberty said disgustedly. 'You're ruining my pie.' She watched as the fleshy, balding old telegraph operator hurried out. Then she gazed about her to see how many of the other diners had been eavesdropping.

As she'd expected — all of them! And, typically, they all quickly looked away as her gaze met theirs.

Go to hell, she thought irritably. *All of you. Just go to hell!*

She cut into the wedge of hot, fresh-baked pie with her fork, scooped up some of the sugary filling with the crust, stuffed it in her mouth, and chewed slowly. But though apple was her favorite of all pies, and she made sure she had a slice with her lunch whenever she came to Guthrie, today her anger made the apples taste bitter and she pushed the plate away.

Rising, she dropped a quarter on the table, picked up her flat-crowned black hat, and stormed out.

2

The Wiley farm, like most small farmsteads in Oklahoma Territory claimed in the '89 Land Run, resembled a remote island in a yellow sea of sunburned prairie. The neighboring farms that had been claimed on the same day were all gone, their once-tilled fields now nothing but rutted, dry red earth dotted with withered shoots — the only reminder of the crops that settlers had hoped would feed them and perhaps even turn a small profit on market day.

By sheer grit and determination the Wiley family had survived those three long years since the Land Run, husband, wife and three children often eating nothing but turnips for weeks on end. Last January it seemed as if their luck had turned; early rains had enabled the fields of cotton and the vegetable garden that surrounded their small sod-roofed shack to flourish, offering the faint possibility of them not only having enough money to buy supplies in the nearest All-Black town of Huttonville but perhaps also to allow them to buy a bolt of cloth that could be turned into clothing for the entire family.

But then the rains had disappeared and now the drought-stricken land was all but dried up, forcing even Vernon Wiley, a plodding, determined, ever-optimistic Negro in his mid-thirties, to wonder if the Good Lord had truly forsaken them.

That morning the endless whimpering of his hungry two-month-old son had driven the former slave out into the cotton fields before dawn in the hopes of seeing or smelling signs of approaching rain. But the pale gray sky was cloudless and the air so dry his clothing crackled with electricity.

He walked along the rows between the shriveled cotton bushes that he'd planted in February and expected to be ready for harvesting in July, and saw little more than dead branches and withered leaves. He sighed wearily, hearing in his head the repeated warnings by white farmers that the soil was not suitable for cotton — and guiltily wondered if the dying crop was God's way of punishing him for his stubborn desire to prove the White Man wrong.

Before he could decide, he heard horses approaching. He turned and saw two riders crossing the prairie toward him. Curious, he studied them carefully. Both looked about thirty, but one was considerably larger than the other. They were dressed like cowboys, but rode more like townsmen, and below high-crowned Stetsons their hard-eyed faces were covered by stubbly beards. They rode at an easy, mile-consuming pace, as if in no hurry to get anywhere, each man leading an extra horse.

There was nothing threatening about them and though they were well-armed, Vernon's only concern was that he had neither coffee nor food to offer them. It so shamed him, he lowered his head and pretended to be examining a bush, hoping they would ride on.

But they didn't. They reined up outside his shack and Vernon had no choice but to leave the cotton field and walk over to them.

'Mornin' to you, sirs,' he said, a life of slavery making him remove his straw hat in the presence of whites. 'Fine day for traveling.'

The larger, younger, better-looking of the two said politely: 'Me 'n my cousin was hopin' you could spare some water for our horses.'

'Ain't much to spare,' Vernon said, thumbing at the near-empty trough alongside his shack, 'but whatever's there you're welcome to use.'

'Thank you kindly,' the younger man said. He nudged his horse toward the trough.

His companion, a small, mean-mouthed man with dead eyes, gave Vernon a long searching stare but made no effort to move.

'Been here long, mister?'

'Since '89, sir.'

'Boomer Sooner, eh?'

'No, sir. I never jumped no gun. Didn't seem like there was a need for it. I wasn't expecting to claim no bottom land. Hundred'n sixty acres of free land anywheres seemed more'n enough good luck for me 'n my family.'

'Beats being in chains, I reckon,' said the small man, Roy McClory. 'They inside?' he added, nodding at the cabin. 'Your family, I mean?'

'Yes, sir.'

'Fetch 'em out here.'

'Sir?'

'You heard me, boy. Get 'em out here so I can see 'em.' As he spoke, he drew his six-gun, thumbed the hammer back and aimed at Vernon.

'Yes, sir! Right away, boss.' Alarmed, Vernon hurried into the shack.

The door closed and Roy heard a wooden bar sliding into position. He smiled contemptuously, as if expecting this, and holstered his Colt. Then, dismounting, he pulled a shotgun from its scabbard under the saddle and signaled to his cousin to join him. Together they approached the shack.

Roy pounded on the door with his fist.

'Go 'way,' Vernon called out. 'We don't want no trouble with no white folks.'

'You already got trouble,' Roy said. 'Open up else you'll make it worse on yourselves.'

'Please, mister. Take all the water you want and leave us be,' Vernon begged.

His words were drowned out by the roar of Roy's shotgun. The door shattered and what was left swung inward.

Inside, a woman and three children screamed in fear.

Travis McClory licked his lips in anticipation and looked pleadingly at his cousin.

'Go ahead,' Roy told him. 'They're all yours.'

Travis flashed a delighted smile and stepped through the door, a Colt .45 in each hand.

Huddled against the far wall was a light-skinned black woman holding a baby in her arms with two young children crouched fearfully beside her.

Their father, Vernon, stood protectively in front of them, armed with a Civil War Springfield musket.

'Stay back,' he warned Travis. 'Please, mister, I don't wanna have to shoot — '

Travis shot him, kept shooting him until both Colts were empty, his smile one of pure insane joy.

3

It was oven-hot outside the Hotel Guthrie. But not as hot as Liberty's fiery temper right now.

Like her father, a former wrangler who went by the name of Drifter, she hated injustice of any kind. Hell, one of the reasons she'd become a lawman was because she wanted to right those injustices; and though she'd been warned by Marshal Thompson, who had appointed her, that being a woman deputy US marshal would be viewed by most men in Oklahoma Territory as a travesty, she'd believed that by performing her duties as well or better than any man, she could overcome their prejudice and eventually win their trust.

That had been nine months ago — nine months of silently enduring the taunting slurs and mocking remarks that, despite her integrity and exemplary record, had come her way and were *still* coming her way; and though she'd never complained or whined about being treated unfairly, emotionally the constant verbal beating was wearing her down and she'd had to fight not to let all the vitriolic criticism make her bitter . . . or worse, quit.

But quitting wasn't in her blood. In that respect she was very similar to her predecessor, a tough, strong-minded young deputy US marshal named Liberty Cahill, who'd endured the same kind of insults and criticism. Undaunted, Cahill had ignored her detractors and had begun to build a reputation as a fair and honest lawman when she was shot down in Mexico.

Liberty had known Cahill and greatly admired her. In fact, she'd so admired her that before taking the oath to become a deputy US marshal, she'd paid homage to the dead lawman by legally changing her name from Emily to Liberty; at the same time promising herself to carry on the fight to prove to everyone that women had a right to be lawmen.

Now, as she stood fuming on the boardwalk, she remembered Marshal Macahan's favorite phrase — 'Caution's the way' — and, taking a deep breath, expelled most of her frustration and anger. What remained she knew would always be with her so long as she wasn't accepted as a legitimate lawman. But she also knew her anger wasn't necessarily a bad thing. It wasn't out of control, and she was determined to not let it impair her judgment or color any of the decisions she might have to make during the days ahead.

Calmer now, she jammed her hat on, low enough so the sun wouldn't get in her eyes, and crossed the street to the marshal's office. There, she wrote a note telling Marshal Thompson where she'd gone and why, propped it up on his desk, and headed to her rented room to pack clothes and toiletries in her saddle-bags.

4

The afternoon train to Clearwater — a small but fast-growing town that was a jumping-off point to neighboring Indian Territory — wasn't full and Liberty got a double seat to herself. Putting her rifle, bedroll, and saddle-bags on the overhead rack, she sat by the window and stretched out her long slim legs.

The train pulled out of the station and gathered speed. Soon all signs of civilization disappeared. Outside, the yellow drought-parched flatlands sped past Liberty's window. She gazed at them for a while, thinking of how green the land around her father's horse ranch outside El Paso must be at that moment. According to his recent letter, west Texas had had an unusually high rainfall that past winter and the normally arid, sunburned prairies, hills, and scrubland were covered in green grass and bright with wildflowers.

Liberty smiled as she pictured all the mares that her father was raising getting fat on the succulent grass, their bellies growing bigger by the month as they prepared to foal in the upcoming spring. It was a pleasing picture, made even more pleasurable by the thought that after she'd arrested the McClory cousins and turned them over to the prison authorities in Guthrie, she planned on asking Marshal Thompson if she could take time off to be with her father during the foaling.

As a child growing up on the Mercer ranch outside Santa Rosa, New Mexico with her mother and her step-father, Pa Mercer, she'd always looked forward to the period from late January to early April, when the foals were born. She hadn't known Drifter was her father then — or that his real name was Quint Longley — and she'd always been puzzled by her deep feelings for the wandering wrangler and couldn't understand why she so looked forward to seeing him whenever he stopped at the ranch to water his horse and eat supper with them.

A sudden thud on the window interrupted her thoughts. She turned quickly, in time to see a bird flutter off, dazed from flying into the glass.

The bird's life-threatening collision reminded her that she was not on a pleasure trip; digging out the wanted poster showing the two McClory cousins, she studied their faces. As she did she heard Marshal Macahan's quiet, fatherly voice saying: 'Spend time looking at the faces of the outlaws you're hunting, Liberty. It will not only help you to recognize them, but, after careful study, will reveal traits of their personality — and knowing those traits might one day be the difference between you living or dying.'

'But killers don't always look like killers,' she'd protested. 'In that picture of William Bonney you showed me, he looked more like a small, shy schoolboy than a renegade suspected of gunning down more than ten men.'

'Hard to tell what the Kid looked like from that tintype,' Macahan cautioned. 'It wasn't only reversed so that he appeared to be left-handed, it made him look buck-toothed and short on brains — none of which was true. Now you take that Wanted poster that was pinned on the wall in Sheriff Forbes' office in Santa Rosa; there's a different story. The fella who drew it had actually seen the Kid in Lincoln and captured the look in his blue squinty eyes — a cold, hard, wintry look warning any experienced lawman that he wasn't pursuing a shy, fun-loving schoolboy.'

Liberty had taken that warning to heart. Now, looking at the faces of Roy and Travis McClory, she studied their eyes and their mouths, looking for hidden traits or signs that might reveal more than the fact that they were murderers.

Both had unruly dark hair and thick, dark eyebrows. But Roy, the older by a year, had a pinched, mean mouth, broken nose and dead eyes. Travis, the bigger of the two, was cowboy handsome and had a wide friendly smile. Her first thought was that it was unusual for outlaws to be shown smiling in Wanted posters — they usually looked grim and threatening.

Then it hit her. If the artist had drawn Travis McClory smiling, surely he must have had a reason? But what was it?

Liberty studied the sketch for a few more minutes then, unable to come to any definite conclusion, memorized the two faces and tucked the poster back into her vest pocket. Normally, she didn't wear a vest — just a denim shirt and pants, blue neckerchief, and brown rough-out boots. But with fall came colder nights calling for either a jacket or vest, along with the yellow slicker she always kept rolled up with her bedroll behind her saddle.

She yawned, more from inactivity than weariness, and turned to the window. Outside the sun-scorched wasteland was still flat and desolate. But the farther southeast the train traveled the more rocks and ravines and dry riverbeds became a part of the landscape.

The heat made her sleepy. Ignoring a fly buzzing about her head, she dozed for a while; then upon waking, took out her Waltham silver pocket watch and saw that it was almost 4 o'clock. That meant they were due in Clearwater in a few minutes. She turned the watch over and studied the engraving on the back.

TO MY DAUGHTER, EMILY
WITH LOVE
DRIFTER

The watch had been a twenty-first birthday gift from her father, who refused to call her anything but Emily. She treasured it, but was bothered by the fact that he hadn't had 'Father' engraved on it instead of his nickname: 'Drifter'.

She knew he loved her and was

proud of her — though wished she'd chosen a less dangerous profession — and often said she was the best thing that ever happened to him. Nor was he shy about admitting she was his daughter, even though everyone knew he'd never been married. So why had he used Drifter instead of Father? *One day*, she thought, yawning, *I'll find the courage to ask him.*

Just then the train began slowing down. Looking out the window she saw the tracks curving toward the outskirts of Clearwater, with its familiar sun-bleached wooden water tower and yellow-and-brown stationhouse facing town. Beyond the town lay open scrubland that stretched all the way to a range of rolling brown hills that made up the distant horizon.

The rural, almost bucolic atmosphere was comforting and made her feel warm inside. Clearwater reminded her of Santa Rosa and all the wonderful memories she'd experienced while growing up with the Mercers. But happiness had its price. Just the thought of the Mercers and their violent death nine years ago by marauding Comancheros filled her with sadness and, as always, she had trouble controlling her mixed emotions.

Yawning again, she rose and got her things down from the overhead rack. Several of the passengers were also preparing to get off the train. Some of them recognized her and smiled warmly. Liberty smiled back and then reached for the hand-tooled leather scabbard containing her Winchester '92. The scabbard and new repeating rifle had been parting gifts from Marshal Macahan on the day he'd told her that she'd been transferred from El Paso to Guthrie, and she treasured them every bit as much as her watch.

Now, looking at the left side of the hand-checkered rifle stock, she read for the umpteenth time the inscription written on a small brass plate: 'Be responsible. Trust yourself.'

Liberty sighed. *I'm trying*, she

thought. *God knows, I'm trying.*

They were almost at the station now. The train gave two long whistle blasts as it slowly chugged alongside the stationhouse and stopped. Liberty let a young couple with two children get off ahead of her then stepped down on to the narrow plank platform and made her way to the last boxcar, which contained her horse.

'I had me a feelin' you'd show up,' a voice drawled behind her.

She turned and saw it was Sheriff Will Hagen. A short, powerfully built man who looked older than his fifty years, he'd been leaning against the side of the stationhouse and she hadn't seen him. She waited for him to approach then said: 'Try not to be too excited, Will. I might get the wrong impression and think you were happy to see me.'

He puffed up indignantly. 'Got no call to talk to me that way, Deputy. When'd I ever throw mud in your face?'

Liberty almost laughed. 'Let me put it another way, Sheriff — when'd you ever back a play of mine? You know, as common courtesy? One law officer to another?'

Sheriff Hagen looked offended. 'If you're still holding a grudge against me for not helping when the Wallace brothers was huntin' you, reckon you've forgotten I had the fever so bad I could barely get out of bed.'

'I haven't forgotten anything,' Liberty said tersely. 'Nor will I. Ever. Now, step aside. I need to get Regret out.' She turned and walked to the last boxcar, where a ramp had already been lowered and a disheveled-looking conductor stood picking straw off his rumpled black uniform while he waited for her to unload her horse.

'I was goin' to bring him out for you, Deputy. But that mule-brained son-of-a-buck tried to bite me and then cow-kicked me, so I figured I'd let you handle him.'

'Wise move,' Liberty said, eyeing the rangy buckskin that was tied up inside. 'Don't take it personally, Mr Stearn.

Dumb lunkhead does the same to me all the time. I swear he doesn't have a friendly bone in his whole damn body.'

'Why do you keep him, then? Sure ain't for his looks.'

'Because he can run from here to Texas without breaking a sweat.'

'Ahh. Yeah, well, you bein' a lawman, I can see how that would come in mighty handy.' He stood back and watched as Liberty climbed the ramp and eased her way around the irascible buckskin, warning it as she did not to mess with her.

Regret, so-named because everyone had told her she'd regret buying him, laid his ears back and took a nip at her. She jumped back, avoiding his teeth. Then balling her gloved hand into a fist, she punched the horse on the soft part of his nose. Startled more than hurt, he whinnied and backed up, allowing her to reach the blanket hanging over the rack beside her saddle.

'We can do this peacefully,' she said as she threw the blanket over the buckskin's back, 'or make a war out of it. Your call.'

Regret snorted and stamped his foreleg, pawing at the straw as if not sure what to do next.

'While you're deciding,' Liberty said, 'I'll get on with my business.'

The buckskin snorted again and kicked the wall behind it.

Liberty ignored its quirky behavior and quickly threw her saddle on its back, kneed it in the belly to force out any excess air, then tightened the cinch and lowered the stirrups. Next she grabbed the bridle, eased the bit between his big yellow teeth and fastened the head straps. The suddenly placid horse made no further attempt to bite or kick her.

'Glad you came to your senses,' she said as she untied the halter rope. 'We've got a long ride ahead of us and — '

Regret suddenly swung his head around, catching her off-guard and knocking her sprawling. The buckskin nickered, then, as calm and precise as a parade horse, trotted down the ramp and stood motionless on the platform.

Liberty got up from the urine-soaked straw and dusted herself off. More embarrassed than angry, she put her hat back on and came to the door.

'You all right, Deputy?' the conductor asked. 'Ain't hurt, are you?'

'I'm fine, thanks.' She hitched up her pants and straightened her gun-belt so that the holstered, cedar-handled Colt .45 sat comfortably on her right hip. 'But if I were a certain horse,' she said, glaring at the buckskin, 'I'd be mighty careful about eating my next meal. Broken glass can be awfully hard to detect when it's mixed in with a bucket of oats.'

As if knowing it was an empty threat the buckskin tossed its head and snorted derisively.

5

Liberty rode along Main Street, in and out of the late-afternoon shadows cast by the stores, saloons, and restaurants lining the boardwalks, to the town hall.

Among the horses tied up outside the large wood-framed building was Sheriff Hagen's gray gelding. She realized he must have ridden straight there the station to speak to the mayor and town fathers.

Whatever he was telling them about her, she knew it wouldn't be flattering. She and the sheriff had bumped heads the first time she'd ridden into Clearwater while tracking down three outlaws who'd robbed the First National Bank in Oklahoma City and then fled into Indian Territory. At the time she'd only been a deputy US marshal for three weeks and Will Hagen, a long-time, set-in-his-ways sheriff at Clearwater, had resented the fact that she answered only to Marshal Thompson and made no attempt to be cooperative or helpful. Worse, he'd ridiculed her behind her back, painting her as an overly ambitious, incompetent girl, barely out of convent school, whose attempt to do a man's job was so futile that it put the townspeople's lives in jeopardy.

Later, when she'd been assigned by Marshal Thompson to Clearwater and had rented a little house there and shared the sheriff's office, Hagen pretended to patch up their differences. But Liberty, distrusting him, had kept her distance and eventually won some of the townspeople's respect by capturing two of the infamous Wallace gang, Josh and Caleb.

Now, as she dismounted and tied her horse to the rail, she nodded politely to two primly dressed spinsters walking past. They were part of the local Women's Christian Temperance Union and, as such, held strong voices in the community. Winning them over, Marshal

Thompson had told her, was imperative if she ever wanted the town on her side.

The sisters nodded back, their severe expressions never changing, and continued on their way. Liberty, feeling as if she'd won a minor victory just by getting them to acknowledge her existence, turned back to her horse, pulled her rifle from its scabbard, and entered the town hall.

Mayor Justin's office was on the ground floor at the rear of the two-story building. Liberty crossed the large reception room where dances and town meetings were held, her boots echoing off the uncarpeted wooden floor, and knocked on the mayor's door. It opened immediately, suggesting that she'd been expected, and Sheriff Hagen asked her to come in.

One look at the expressions facing her told her she was right: the town council was waiting for her. Feeling as if she were entering a room full of coiled rattlesnakes, Liberty defiantly kept her hat on and walked up to the mayor's large, imposing desk.

Behind it sat Mayor Robert 'Bob' Justin, while seated on either side of him were the members of the council. She recognized most of them: Tom Akins, once a desk clerk but now manager of the Hotel Independence; Luke Logan, owner of the livery stable; Ed Willard, the barber; Walt Neuhauser, the blacksmith; Stu Wexler, the mortician; Dr Bryce Masters, and two other men she guessed had recently been elected.

Without waiting for Sheriff Hagen to take his seat, she dispensed with civilities and said tersely: 'I'm sure Will has told all of you why I'm here, gentlemen, so I'll get right to the meat. Do any of you have information that might help me find or capture Roy or Travis McClory?'

'No,' began Sheriff Hagen. 'But — '

Mayor Justin stopped him. 'Will, if you don't mind, this is my office and as such, I'll do the talking.'

'S-Sure, Bob . . . ' The sheriff sat

34

down like a scolded schoolboy and nervously toyed with the brim of his Stetson.

'Now,' the mayor said to Liberty, 'to answer your question, deputy, no, none of us has any information about the McClory brothers.'

'Cousins, not brothers.'

'Whatever. Either way, we have no information regarding their where-abouts. And that's final.'

His tone was pompous and dogmatic and she knew he was enjoying himself by putting this feisty, quick-tempered young woman in her place.

'Thank you, Bob . . . ' Liberty smiled — a thin, dangerous smile that chilled the mayor. 'Then I won't waste any more of your time.' She nodded respect-fully at the other men, 'Gentlemen,' and started out.

'Wait,' Neuhauser said. 'There was one thing.'

'What's that, Walt?'

'Whyn't you tell her, Luke?' the large, slab-shouldered blacksmith said to the hostler. 'You're the one who told me.'

Luke Logan, a small, taciturn man whose gray chin whiskers were stained by tobacco juice, looked at Liberty with watery, red-rimmed eyes but didn't say anything.

'I'd appreciate hearing whatever it is, Mr Logan,' she said, hoping to coax the old hostler into speaking. 'And I promise you, it'll go no further.'

Logan tongued his chew from one cheek to the other before saying: 'Heard it from a stranger, day 'fore yesterday. He and this other fella was watering their horses outside my place, talking 'bout the McClorys. Said they hoped to meet up with 'em sometime tomorrow. That'd be today, of course — '

'Dammit,' exploded the mayor, 'how come you never told me this, Luke?'

'Let him speak his piece, Bob,' Liberty snapped, sharply enough to silence the mayor and widen the eyes of the other men. 'Go on, Mr Logan,' she continued. 'Did these men say where they hoped to meet up with the McClorys?'

'Yep. Violet Springs.'

Everyone's eyebrows arched in alarm.

'You won't be wanting to go there, Deputy,' warned Doc Masters. 'Not unless you're itching to get buried. I mean it ain't called Hell Town for nothing.'

Liberty didn't say anything. But the mention of the wildest of all the whiskey towns — so-called because they were often nothing more than a saloon and a cemetery — built along the boundary dividing Oklahoma Territory and the Seminole Nation, unnerved her. Momentarily her resolve faltered and she considered discontinuing her search for the McClory cousins.

Then she saw Sheriff Hagen smirking and it made her mad enough to say quietly: 'Thank you, Mr Logan. I appreciate the tip.' With a polite nod to the other men, she walked out of the office.

Someone came hurrying after her. 'Liberty, hold up!'

She turned and saw it was Bryce Masters. 'What is it, Doc?'

37

'I meant what I said in there — you show your face in Violet Springs, you're signing your own death warrant.'

'What else would you have me do — slink home with my tail between my legs?'

'Well, no, but . . . dammit, at least deputize someone to back you up.'

'Like, who? Marshal Thompson's busy at a murder trial in Tulsa and I'm safer off riding alone than with Sheriff Hagen.'

The doctor, a small, squat man of sixty who'd taken a Confederate musket ball in his left leg and limped thereafter, gave a disgusted snort. 'Hagen's a gutless fool. We all know that. Only reason he's sheriff is 'cause nobody else wants the job.'

'Then who're you recommending — yourself?'

'Not me. I got too many folks relying on me to deliberately get myself shot up.'

'Who, then?'

'Marshal Macahan.'

'That's an odd choice, considering he's in El Paso.'

'A wire gets him here by tomorrow evening, latest. Can't you at least wait that long in order to save your life?'

'I won't deny that I'd like him with me, Doc. But I knew what I was getting into when I took the oath, and I can't be calling for help every time I run into danger.'

'What about the fella who helped you track down the Wallace gang?'

'Flowers? He's a railroad detective — the McClorys haven't robbed any trains that I know of.'

'Then how about — ?'

She angrily cut him off. 'Don't say it, Doc. My father's a horse rancher, not a lawman.'

'Maybe so, but there's very few folks can jerk an iron faster than Drifter or shoot as straight.'

'And I'm not one of them, right?'

'Dammit, I never said that. I've never seen you slap leather but I know your pa must've taught you well. And I'm sure you've practised — '

'But practice can only take you so far — that what you're trying to tell me?'

'No, I — '

'Well, you're right, Doc. Through my father and Marshal Macahan I've met a lot of gunmen and they all agree on one thing: practise can teach you to hit what you're aiming at, but it can't make you any faster on the draw than your reflexes will allow. Slow reflexes, slow draw — fast reflexes, fast draw.' She paused, her mind traveling back to her teenage years, then said: 'Everyone agrees that Latigo Rawlins was the fastest who ever lived. Know how often he practiced? Never. I know. I was once in love with him. And when I asked him why he was so fast, he said he was born fast. Said it was a gift. Something he could just do better than anyone else. But like Marshal Macahan's always saying, there's more to being a marshal than jerking a gun.'

'I know that, Liberty, and I'm not trying to belittle — '

'Forget it, Doc. Either I'm capable of doing my job or I'm not. I think I am. I sure hope I am, anyway. But if I'm wrong — well, at least I tried.'

'I'll make sure that's written on your headstone.'

'Thanks for the vote of confidence.'

Doc Masters shook his head, vexed by her stubbornness. 'I admire you, Liberty. Always have. Got sand *and* brains. But goddammit, girl, this time you're going off half-cocked. Hell, you go to Violet Springs and you'll end up like your namesake — dead 'fore you can make your mark.'

'So be it.' Liberty shrugged and turned to leave. Then a thought hit her and she looked back at him. 'Mind if I ask you something personal?'

'Go ahead.'

'You're one of the few men who's never thrown his name into the hat when the question of women lawmen came up — why is that, Doc?'

'Mean do I agree with the idea?' He shrugged his narrow shoulders. 'If a woman can be a doctor or a lawyer, like some are back East, seems to me they can also be a lawman. I'll tell you this, though — I'd raise holy hell if one of my daughters even so much as hinted she wanted to wear a badge.'

'Fair enough,' Liberty said. 'Now, if it's OK with you, Doc, I'd best be making dust. It's a fair ride from here to Violet Springs.' Tipping her hat, she turned and walked out.

Doc Masters sighed, more frustrated than angry, and then returned to the mayor's office.

6

From that very first summer day in 1891 when a saloon had been built on claimed land near the South Canadian River and alongside Indian Territory, violence became as common as trail dust.

Originally called Violet because of the wild violets growing profusely in the area, and later known as Violet Springs for the nearby springs, the tiny tent-town was unique in the fact that at the east end of Main Street there was a gated barbed-wire fence marking the legal boundary separating Oklahoma Territory from the Seminole Nation.

The town was lawless from the start. There were so many shootings between drunken cowboys, gunmen, outlaws and rowdy liquored-up Indians that inevitably ended in death that it soon earned the nickname: Hell Town. But frequent as the violence was initially, months later when a second saloon was built opposite the first, sparking a rivalry, it immediately increased — until it wasn't unusual for five or six men to be killed on a daily basis, their bodies then unceremoniously buried in the walled cemetery overlooking the cottonwoods, plum thickets, and wild berries growing along the banks of the river.

Now, a year or so later as the McClory cousins rode into Violet Springs, the tents had been replaced by makeshift shacks, sod houses, and a row of false-fronted wooden buildings housing a livery stable, barbershop, undertaker, blacksmith, whorehouse, restaurant and a general store stocked with stolen goods.

The McClorys tied their horses up outside the Bottom Dollar, grabbed their rifles and walked to the entrance. Inside, they could hear raucous laughter mingled with a tinny player-piano. Peering over the batwing doors they saw the saloon was crowded with half-breeds, whores, drifters, and hard, ruthless killers, whose

faces adorned Wanted posters throughout the territory.

'I don't see 'em,' Travis said. 'Do
you?'

Roy shook his head. 'Could be
they're upstairs beddin' whores. But I
doubt it 'cause their horses would most
likely be tied up outside.'

Travis looked across the street at the
livery stable. The double doors were
open and he could see several horses
stalled inside. 'Not in there, neither. Maybe
they ain't comin'?' he said hopefully.

'Quit dreamin', for chrissake. The
Dunns are comin' after us, all right.
They'll be here sure as there's fires in
hell. Just a matter of time 'fore the
bastards show up is all. And I aim to
spend that time cuddlin' up to a jug full
of joy-juice and a leg-spreading woman
big as a mattress.'

'Named Ellie Rose?'

Roy nodded, grinned and spat into
the dirt. He then pushed the doors
aside and entered the noisy, smoke-
filled saloon, his cousin following.

Their entrance was magnetic; everyone stopped what they were doing and stared at them — even the men playing poker at the tables at the rear.

Unfazed, the McClorys stared back at the wary, suspicious faces as they walked to the crude plank bar as if defying anyone to challenge them. When no one did they ordered whiskey from the large, brutal-faced barkeep, Bart Morris, then told him to leave the jug and settled down to drinking.

The tension faded in the crowded saloon. Realizing that the two men weren't lawmen or bounty hunters, everyone shrugged off their suspicions and went back to what they were doing.

All except one brassy-looking whore with straggly brown hair, tired, boozy eyes, and a knife scar that disfigured her left cheek — one look at the newcomers and she jumped up, screaming fearfully: 'It's them! It's them I tell ya! The McClorys! The fellas who cut me!'

As everyone turned, startled, and looked at her, she stumbled away from the bar, pointing wildly at the McClorys. 'Dirty lousy bastards!' she yelled. 'I'll teach you to take a knife to me!'

Grabbing a pistol from the holster of one of the poker players, she fired at Travis. In her panic, she missed him. And before she could pull the trigger again, Roy shot her with his rifle.

The bullet punched a hole in the whore's ample cleavage and she collapsed in a heap.

Roy coldly shot her twice more to make sure she was dead, then swung around and leveled his Winchester at the crowd facing him.

'Anyone else want in on this?' he asked grimly. Then when no one responded: 'For what it's worth, my cousin and me ain't never seen that lyin' bitch afore.'

'Never,' Travis said, adding to the lie. 'Hell, she don't even look like no other whore we ever whored with.'

Again, no one moved or spoke.

Then, 'No one's doubtin' you, friend,' said the barkeep. He was holding the scattergun he'd grabbed from under the bar, both barrels aimed at the McClorys. 'Fact is we don't give a polecat's ass either way. Right, boys?' he said to the crowd.

Yells of, 'Right!' confirmed he was telling the truth.

'Then what's the problem?' Roy demanded.

'The problem, friend, is you still killed her. And 'cause of that, you owe me for what she's worth.'

'Worth?' Roy scoffed. 'That sorry sack of dog puke ain't worth spit.'

'Maybe not to you. But to me she's worth what she would've earned in the weeks or months to come.'

'Who says an ugly, scarred-up bitch like that would've earned you a damned nickel?' Travis said, hand hovering over his gun.

'I says, mister. She's been whorin' for me since this place opened, and a tidy sum she's earned. And 'less you want me to blast a hole clean through you, sonny, keep your hand 'way from that iron.'

'Do it,' Roy said when Travis didn't move. 'We got enough on our plate right now without piling on seconds.'

Grudgingly, Travis obeyed.

Satisfied, Morris said: 'Now, you fellas owe me fifty in gold and I'll be seein' it afore you take another breath.'

He cocked both hammers back on the big gun, and everyone directly behind the McClorys scattered.

'That's the price of dog puke down here, huh?' Roy said.

'Reckon so.'

Roy shrugged. 'Well, I ain't one to buck a trend, but forty's as high as I'll go.'

'Let's see the money afore I agree.'

Roy reached inside his shirt.

'Easy,' Morris warned.

Roy slowly withdrew his hand, showing a small pouch that he shook to let the barkeep know it contained coins. Then with all eyes on him, he loosened the string and dumped a handful of double eagles on to the bar.

Pushing two of them toward the

barkeep, he went to stuff the other gold coins back into the pouch.

'Did I say fifty — I meant sixty,' Morris said. Grinning, he used the double-barrel of the shotgun to guide a third coin alongside the first two.

'Nice little business you got here,' Roy said grudgingly. 'Reckon I won't be shootin' no more whores from now on.' Picking up his pouch and the jug he turned to Travis, adding: 'Time we was movin' on, cousin.'

Travis gulped the last of his drink and hurried after Roy.

Morris pocketed the double eagles and then turned to the crowd.

'Whiskey's on me, boys.'

Shouting their approval, everyone surged up to the bar.

7

It was dark when Liberty rode up to the Wiley farm and she was surprised not to see a light shining in the window. Wondering if the family had finally called it quits and abandoned their holdings, she reined up at the half-open gate fronting the little sod-roof shack and looked cautiously about her.

Though nothing appeared to be wrong, it wasn't like Vernon Wiley to leave his gate open and she sat there a moment in the saddle, trying to ignore the uneasy feeling running through her.

After a little while she nudged the buckskin forward, the horse bumping aside the gate, and rode up to the front of the shack. Immediately she saw the remains of the door hanging from one of its leather hinges and quickly drew her Colt. Standing up in the stirrups, she peered closer, straining to see inside the shack. But all she saw was darkness. Ready to shoot anything that was threatening, she slowly dismounted and approached the shattered door.

'Mr Wiley,' she called out. 'You in there?'

Silence.

'Mr Wiley, it's me — Deputy Marshal Mercer. Can you hear me?'

More silence — except for the chirping of hidden crickets.

Liberty dug out one of the half-dozen wooden matches she always kept in her shirt pocket. Never taking her eyes off the dark interior of the shack, she struck the match on the door jamb.

The match flared, brightening the darkness, and Liberty held it out in front of her as she slowly entered the shack.

The sight confronting her was so horrific it made her gag. Dropping the still-burning match she stumbled outside. There, bent double, she retched for a few moments before managing to calm her stomach and her emotions.

Then she struck another match and forced herself to go back into the shack. Sickened by the sight of the dead and mutilated bodies, she looked around for any signs that might prove the murderers were savages. But there was no trace of a broken feather or war paint, and none of the bodies had arrows in them, and gradually she was forced to admit that maybe Indians hadn't done this.

Obviously, though, a struggle had taken place. Blood was spattered on the walls, furniture was overturned and a shattered hurricane lamp lay on the floor. The pantry had been ransacked for food and the contents of drawers were scattered everywhere.

Liberty flared another match and entered the bedroom. The sight of Vera Wiley, dead and bloodied on the bed, obviously raped, made Liberty's stomach jerk. Managing not to vomit, she started out then stopped as she saw the shawl-wrapped infant lying in the home-made crib. Teeth gritted, she turned the baby over, its cold flesh verifying that it was dead, and realized that the blood on it must have come from the mother, since the child seemed to be unharmed. Guessing that it had been suffocated, she steeled herself and flared another match — holding it high in order to give the room a final look.

There was no blood on the walls but someone had smeared some on a cheap wooden crucifix hanging above the bed, so that it dripped from the hands and feet of the tortured Christ.

Liberty stared at it in dismay until the dying match burned her fingers.

Then she ran out.

Outside, she gulped down mouthfuls of cool night air until she no longer felt like heaving; then she gazed heavenward and for the first time in her young life — certainly since entering the convent — questioned if God really existed; and if He did, how He could allow something so senselessly cruel and inhuman to happen to gentle, kind folks like the Wileys.

Equally hard to accept was the idea that this gruesome atrocity hadn't been committed by drunken renegade Comanches or Kiowas, as she'd first thought, but instead by people of her own kind — *white men* — the McClorys!

What possessed the souls of such murderers, she wondered, that could drive them to wantonly butcher innocent families, apparently just for the hell of it? Even ruthless gunmen like Latigo Rawlins or John Wesley Hardin needed to be antagonized in some way before they gunned someone down!

Sickened and unable to make herself go back inside, Liberty hurried to the cotton field. Gathering armfuls of dead bushes she spread them all around the shack. She then said a few words of prayer for the souls of the Wiley family, flared her last match, and set fire to the dry wood. It caught fire instantly and soon a wall of flames engulfed the shack.

Liberty stood there long enough to ensure that the raging fire would turn everything to ashes . . . then mounted and rode slowly eastward in the direction of Violet Springs.

8

In a dark alley beside the livery stable, opposite the saloon, Roy and Travis McClory waited grimly for the barkeep to come out.

According to the blacksmith they'd spoken to earlier, Bart Morris always quit at three in the morning, ate a burned steak and a double portion of pan-fried potatoes, washed everything down with a tall beer, and then went home.

It was now 3.30 a.m. and the saloon was almost empty. The few men remaining were so drunk they needed the support of whores or friends in order to walk outside. Others, who'd passed out in the saloon, were being tossed into the street by Morris's helper, a big, muscular former slave named Moses, who mopped the floor and emptied the spittoons. Still others emerged on their own power, clutching jugs of whiskey, whooping it up and shooting off their guns.

The McClorys had been waiting there for over an hour and Roy was growing angrier by the minute. He drained the jug of whiskey and hurled it away. The jug shattered, shards flying everywhere, making their horses stir uneasily.

'When he does come out,' Travis said eagerly, 'do I get him first?'

'No. This bastard's mine!'

Travis looked disappointed but knew better than to argue with his ill-tempered cousin. Facing front, he watched as two riders wearing trail dusters and with their hats pulled down low against the wind-blown dust came out of the night and approached along Main Street.

Both were white and young, Travis noted, but the slimmer of the two had raven-black hair poking from under her hat and her dark-eyed, narrow, angular face had been burned brown as tobacco by the sun. Her companion was also tanned but there all resemblance ended. As beautiful as any woman, he was small but well-proportioned, had long golden hair that curled over his collar, and large, deep-set eyes that were as blue as a summer sky.

Reining up outside the Bottom Dollar, the riders dismounted and tied up their horses, shook the trail dirt from their dusters, and entered the saloon.

Watching them, Travis wondered if the short, yellow-haired rider was actually a woman posing as a man. Before he could decide, two drunken half-breeds came staggering out of the saloon. They had trouble walking and after a few steps, the larger of the two tripped over a cowboy who'd passed out in the street. Stumbling, the 'breed lost his balance and went sprawling in the dirt. When he got up he was covered in wet horse dung. Enraged, he stood there cursing and kicking the unconscious cowboy. The other 'breed tried to drag him away, but the bigger man pushed him aside and continued kicking the cowboy.

Shortly, a second cowboy approached from the corral, leading two saddled horses. Seeing the 'breed kicking his partner, he jerked his six-gun, shouting, 'Damn you, you no-good copper-skin devil,' and fired three times.

The big 'breed crumpled, dead before he hit the dirt.

The other 'breed turned to run, but the cowboy callously gunned him down before he'd taken two steps.

Holstering his Colt, the cowboy dragged his partner to his feet and shook him until the man regained his wits. 'Time to ride, Hal . . . ' Helping his partner step up into the saddle, he then mounted his own horse and together they rode off into the darkness.

Meanwhile, hearing the shots, Morris and his helper, Moses, came to the door of the saloon. Peering cautiously over the batwing doors, they saw the corpses in the street and the cowboys riding off, and stepped outside.

'Go see if they got any money on 'em, Mose,' Morris said, 'or anything else worth taking.' He went back inside.

Moses hurried over to the two corpses, knelt beside each one and searched their pockets. Empty. But one had a hunting knife and the other, the bigger man, had two gold front teeth. Holding the knife like a hammer the ex-slave smashed the teeth from the gums, and dug them out of the dead 'breed's mouth.

As Moses stood up, Morris came out of the saloon and met him halfway. Moses gave him the bloodstained gold teeth. Morris bit on them, nodded to show they were indeed gold, and grinned at the large black man.

'Fair night's haul, eh, Mose?'

'Yes, sir, Mr Morris. Ain't often a fella gets his hands on double eagles an' gold teef.'

'Here, boy, take this,' Morris pressed one of the gold teeth into Moses's hand. 'Consider it wages for this month.'

Moses beamed, all eyes and teeth. 'Thank you kindly, Mr Morris, sir. You a right generous boss.'

'Make sure you turn out all the lamps 'fore you close up,' Morris reminded him, and walked off.

Watching from the alley Roy waited until Moses had entered the saloon before telling Travis: 'Get that gold tooth from him.'

'Then what?'

'Then nothin'. Just wait here till I get back.' Roy hurried off after the barkeep.

Bart Morris lived in a one-room shack a short distance from the saloon. As he walked past the only corral in town he took out a cigar, bit off the end, flared a match on the fence, and paused to light up. The flame fluttered in the pre-dawn breeze blowing in from Indian Territory. Morris turned his back to the wind, sheltering the flame, and lit his cigar. Once the tip was aglow, he flipped the match away and continued walking.

That's when Roy's knife, a long-bladed Arkansas toothpick, slammed into his back.

Morris grunted with pain, cigar dropping to the ground, and reached back in a desperate attempt to pull out the knife. Before he could, Roy came up close behind him and kicked his legs out from under him.

The burly barkeep stumbled and fell to his knees.

'Yes, sir,' Roy said mockingly, 'you surely got a good business goin' here.'

Morris' eyes bugged. 'Y-You,' he gasped.

'Too bad you ain't gonna live long enough to enjoy it.'

'I-I'll pay you,' Morris began — then dribbling blood, he doubled over, head on his knees.

Roy grinned and strutted, rooster-like, in front of the dying man.

'I'll take my double eagles back now,' he crowed, 'seein' as how you got no need for 'em anymore.'

Morris cursed him and struggled to straighten up.

'Here,' Roy said, 'let me help you, friend.' He jerked the knife out of the barkeep's back, held the blade under the man's chin and slit his throat.

Morris pitched forward on to the dirt.

Roy wiped the blood from the blade on the barkeep's shirt and slid the knife back in its sheath. He then searched Morris's pockets, collected his double eagles, some folding money, and the remaining gold tooth. Then, whistling cheerfully, he headed back to the alley alongside the livery stable.

9

When Liberty was still a mile or so from Violet Springs she saw smoke rising from a campfire among some rocks ahead. Dawn was still an hour away and it was too dark to see who occupied the camp, but she was able to make out the silhouettes of two horses tied up near the fire.

Taking out her rifle, she levered in a round then rested the Winchester across the saddlehorn and nudged the buckskin forward. When she was close enough to be heard, she reined up and called out: 'Hey — you in the camp — this is Deputy US Marshal Liberty Mercer. I'm riding in.'

'Come ahead,' a man's voice replied. 'But come slow an' make sure we can see your hands.'

Obeying his instructions, Liberty kept both hands visible and rode slowly into the camp.

Two rough-looking, shabbily clad men with flint-hard eyes appeared from behind the rocks. Both held rifles and kept them aimed at Liberty.

Recognizing them, she shook her head in amused disgust, said: 'Figures. Where there's a dollar to be made the Dunn brothers are always within shouting distance.'

''Be goddamned . . . ' Bill, the oldest of the brothers, lowered his rifle as he recognized Liberty. 'So you're after the reward money, too?'

'I'm after Roy and Travis McClory,' she corrected. 'Lawmen don't qualify for rewards, in case you've forgotten.'

'That's too bad,' he grinned. 'Maybe you should throw away that badge an' become a bounty hunter like me 'n Bee, here.'

Liberty dismounted and joined the brothers at the fire. 'Think you know how I feel about bounty hunters, Mr Dunn.'

'Lower than vermin, if I remember correctly?'

Before she could reply, Bee Dunn said hotly: 'We got us a legal right to capture or kill the McClorys, same as you.'

'She ain't disputin' that, are you, Marshal?' Bill said.

'Nope.' Liberty smiled humorlessly. 'But I am disputing the idea of using the word 'legal' in connection with you or any of your brothers or relatives.'

Bill chuckled. 'I'd take offense to that, 'cept we Dunns never lose sleep over what other folks say or think of us — 'specially when it comes from a lawman.'

'Just as well,' Liberty said. 'Last sheriff I ran into claimed you and your brothers were back to rustling cattle — again.'

'That's a damn lie,' Bee said. 'We're honest businessmen. Got ourselves a meat market in Pawnee and a boarding house outside of Ingalls, you know that.'

'Sure I do,' Liberty said. 'I also know that most of your beef is wearing other folks' brands and all your guests are outlaws' — she ticked off her fingers — 'Bill Doolin, Bitter Creek Newcomb, Daltons, Dynamite Dick Clifton, Little Bill Raider — '

'You make it sound like we invited 'em,' Bill growled.

'Didn't you?'

'Hell, no. They just showed up at our road ranch and naturally we was obliged to be hospitable.'

'Naturally.'

'They didn't even tell us their real names.'

'Surprise, surprise.'

'Go ahead,' Bee said. 'Mock us all you want, Marshal — '

'*Deputy Marshal.*'

'Lots of folks stay at our place without sayin' who they really are,' Bill said. 'We don't question 'em and we don't care about their past. Way we figure, it ain't up to us to nose around in other folks' affairs.'

'Wouldn't be good for business,' Bee said. 'Hell, just so's they pay their tab, that's all we care about.'

'By God, we wouldn't even mind if you stayed there,' Bill said.

Liberty laughed, despite herself. 'Be careful what you wish for, Mr Dunn. One day you might find yourself having to eat those words.'

The brothers swapped uneasy looks and fell silent. For a few moments the only sounds in the night were the crackling of the fire mingled with the faint yipyipping of coyotes. Then Bill poured himself some coffee and held the blackened pot up to Liberty, saying: 'Thirsty, Deputy?'

'Thanks.' Going to her horse, she took a chipped porcelain mug from her saddle-bag. As she did, the buckskin tried to nip her. She jumped back, avoiding his teeth, and glared at him. 'You want to eat tonight or get your ears pinned back?'

Regret showed his teeth again, but made no further attempt to bite her.

'Sweet-tempered devil, ain't he?' Bee said.

Liberty nodded and studied the buckskin as if she were still trying to figure him out. 'It's hard to believe,' she said, returning to the fire where Bill poured her coffee, 'but he's actually mellowed a little since I first bought him. Time was, when he'd kick me at the same time he was trying to bite me. But I've leaned on him some since then and I think I've finally gotten it through his thick skull that I won't tolerate such irascibility.'

'Reckon I wouldn't tolerate it neither,' Bill said, 'if'n I knowed what the deuce it meant.'

'Bad behavior. *Unacceptable* behavior.'

'Uh-huh . . . ' He mulled over her words, said wryly: 'Schoolin' . . . it's a white man's gift and a mighty useful gift it is.'

'I'm beginning to wonder,' Liberty said, thinking aloud, 'lately, the way people have responded to my remarks has made me feel like I was speaking a foreign language.'

'Tried patience, have you?'

'Patience?'

'Yep. Patience is a red man's gift but it's a mighty useful gift, too.'

Liberty sighed. ' 'Fraid I'm not long on patience, Mr Dunn.'

'To be expected.'

'It is?'

'Sure. Folks with schoolin' got no use for patience. Patience just slows 'em down — gets in the way of what they're after.'

'Nonsense. You can't make sweeping statements like that. I mean, why would an uneducated person need more patience?'

'Gives 'em time to catch on to what smart folks is sayin'.'

Liberty stared silently at him, wondering if he was serious.

'Chew or dip?'

'W-What?'

Bill wagged a plug of chewing tobacco at her. 'Chew?'

'Oh, no thanks.'

He bit off a chunk, tongued it into

71

his cheek, handed the plug to his brother and turned to Liberty. 'This problem you got with your horse?'

'What about it?'

'Plain and simple, you want him to quit fightin' you and let hisself get bossed around?'

'I wouldn't put it that way, but, well — I suppose — something like that, yes.'

'Makes no sense if sense is what you're tryin' to make of it.'

'You've lost me, Mr Dunn.'

'Well . . . ' he spat between his boots, 'from what I hear, that buckskin can run the legs off most horses an' it purely don't make sense for a lawman to break the spirit of a horse that can chase the wind.'

Liberty frowned, surprised. 'Who told you Regret could run like that?'

The brothers swapped amused looks, then Bill said: 'When it comes to lawmen, us Dunns make it our business to know all we can 'bout them.'

'Know your enemy, huh?'

'That who you are,' Bee barked, 'our enemy?'

'I hope not,' Liberty said. She finished her coffee and held the mug upside down over the glowing embers, the dregs causing them to spit and hiss. 'I've never had a reason to dislike you or any of your kin. And I'd like to keep it that way.'

'So would we,' Bill said. 'Us Dunns ain't the trouble-makers we're made out to be. Sure, we've had our run-ins with the law, but we ain't near as bad as most folks paint us. Ask Drifter. We've always gotten along when he's come to Ingalls to chase the rabbit — so it wouldn't be neighborly to have hard feelings for his daughter, even if she does wear a badge.'

Liberty looked surprised. 'I didn't know you knew my father.'

'Sure. Him *and* that outlaw he used to ride with, Mesquite Jennings.'

'Mean Gabriel Moonlight?'

'Reckon. Though being on the run, he didn't use his real name back then.

Mesquite Jennings was the only handle we knew him by.' Pausing, he thought a moment before adding: 'There was another fella sometimes rode with 'em, a shootist who was a real fancy dresser — '

'Latigo Rawlins?'

'That'd be him,' said Bill. 'Sawed-off little Texan. Could jerk an iron faster than anybody I ever knowed.'

'That's definitely Latigo.'

'Mean little snot. Heard he once shot a fella for callin' him Shorty.'

'He was a bounty hunter too,' put in Bee.

'I know,' Liberty said sadly. 'It's one of the few things I disliked about him.'

'I'm surprised you knew him at all, you bein' a lawman and all.'

'I wasn't a lawman then. I was just out of school. Besides, he was my father's friend and he treated me well.'

Bill eyed her curiously. 'I heard that too. Heard you might've even been sweet on him — that true?'

Liberty shrugged. 'When you're young

like I was, who knows what your heart's saying.'

Bill chuckled. 'Hedgin' your bets, huh?'

Liberty smiled ruefully but didn't say anything.

Bee said: 'Love or no love, it don't change nothin'. It's still mighty suspicious you knowing so many gunmen who had run-ins with the law.'

'Luck of the draw, according to my father.'

'What if it wasn't luck at all?' Bill said.

'Meaning?'

'What if Drifter knew all along it might come in handy some day?'

Liberty frowned. 'If something's chewing on you, Mr Dunn, spit it out.'

'Now, now, no need to get salty, Deputy.'

'Then say what you damn well mean.'

He looked long and hard at her before saying: 'If me 'n Bee was to tell you where the McClorys are holed up and then helped you round 'em up — would you let us take the credit?'

'Why would I do that?'

''Cause there's two of them and only one of you. If we was to throw in with you, then it'd be three against two. Difference could mean your life.'

''Sides,' Bee added, 'you just said lawmen don't get to collect no rewards, so it ain't like we're cheatin' you out of the two thousand dollars.'

'I suppose not,' said Liberty. 'Trouble is from then on folks would be throwing it in my face that I needed bounty hunters in order to do my job. And I already got more than enough detractors as it is. I mean, Judas, there's times when I feel like a red-hot horseshoe being hammered into shape on an anvil.'

'In other words,' Bill said, 'you plan on arrestin' the McClorys by your lonesome?'

'That's my intention, yes.'

He sighed heavily and shrugged at his younger brother.

Liberty saw something in their eyes that warned she was in trouble.

'Hold on,' she said. 'Don't do something you'll later regret.'

'We already done that,' Bill said, 'by lettin' you enter our camp.' He was moving as he spoke and so was Bee. Before Liberty realized what was going on, they'd jumped her, their combined weight knocking her down and pinning her to the ground. She struggled and reached for her Colt, but Bill cold-cocked her with his pistol.

The Dunns looked at the young deputy US marshal sprawled out cold before them, then at each other.

'Sure wisht we hadn't had to do that,' Bill said. 'Word ever leaks out what we done, we'll have thunder an' lightning doggin' us.'

'Maybe we'd be smart to ride away from this?' Bee said.

'From what?'

'Killing her. Two thousand's a mountain of money, but — '

'Don't be a damn' fool,' Bill snapped.

'We ain't goin' to kill her. First off I admire her grit too much, and second, that'd be inviting Drifter and Marshal Macahan to come after us. And I'd sooner jump into hell blindfolded with both hands tied than have those widow-makers on our trail.'

'What, then?'

'We're goin' to tie her up an' take her with us — use her as bait to draw out the McClorys in Hell Town.'

Bee whistled softly. 'Goddamn,' he said, clapping his brother on the back, 'if that ain't a doozy of an idea then I ain't never heard one.'

10

When Liberty came around she found herself gagged, tied hand and foot, and lying on her bedroll, her saddle for a pillow. She looked toward the fire and saw Bill Dunn seated, cross-legged, smoking across from her. Next to him his brother lay snoring under a blanket, boots poking out the bottom.

Liberty tried to talk but the gag limited her to unintelligible grunts.

Bill looked at her, took a final drag on his hand-rolled and flipped the butt into the dying fire. 'You brung this on yourself, Deputy. Me 'n Bee, we tried to reason with you, but . . . ' He paused as Liberty tried to say something, then silencing her with a wave of his hand, said, 'If I remove that gag, will you give me your word not to make a fuss?'

Liberty thought about it for a moment then grudgingly nodded.

Bill got up and kneeled beside her, reached behind her head and unknotted his grimy red kerchief.

Liberty glared at him. 'I'm willing to overlook this, Mr Dunn, if you untie me — right now!'

'Will you throw in with us if'n I do?'

'Absolutely not.'

'Suit yourself.' Bill returned to his side of the fire.

About to erupt, Liberty thought, *Caution's the way*, and restraining her temper, said calmly: 'For someone who says he's a friend of my father, Mr Dunn, you certainly have a strange way of showing it.'

'Could say the same about you,' he growled. 'Refusin' to throw in with us — how friendly's that? 'Specially when we're willin' to split the money three ways.'

'Sure,' Liberty said disgustedly. 'I wager you'd even pay me a visit after I go to jail for taking a bribe.' Before he could respond, she rolled over so that her back was facing him and said no more.

* * *

Come sunup Bill kicked his brother awake. Yawning, Bee relieved himself behind the rocks. He then fixed coffee and heated up the previous night's leftovers while Bill convinced Liberty not to try to escape if he untied her.

'What about my gun?' she asked, as she rubbed the circulation back into her hands. 'You can't expect me to ride into a hell hole like Violet Springs unarmed.'

'And you can't expect me to give you a gun knowin' you might shoot us first chance you got.'

'That'll never happen,' she promised. 'You have my word on it.'

Bill studied her then looked at his brother.

'Your call,' Bee said. 'But if'n it was me, big brother, I wouldn't be givin' no pistol to a marshal who don't want us to get the reward.'

'I never said I didn't want you to get it,' Liberty corrected. 'I just said I can't throw in with you — not so long as I'm wearin' this badge.'

'What if you wasn't wearin' it?' Bill asked. 'How would you feel 'bout us helpin' you then?'

Liberty sighed. 'Same.'

'But you just said different.'

'No, no — I was using my badge as a metaphor.' Seeing that they didn't understand what she meant, she added: 'I meant if I weren't a lawman.'

'Then I ain't givin' you no gun,' Bill said.

'You may as well kill me now, then. Because the moment word leaks out that I'm a deputy US marshal — an *unarmed* deputy US marshal — that border trash is going to be lining up to get first shot at me.' Going to her saddle-bags, she opened one — only to hear a hammer being thumbed back.

'Don't make me shoot you, girl,' Bill said grimly.

Liberty turned and held up something wrapped in a cloth. 'Hardtack,' she explained. 'Thought I'd repay you for the beans and coffee.'

The Dunn brothers grinned sheep-
ishly and holstered their six-guns.

11

After breakfast and rolling a smoke they kicked dirt over the fire, mounted up, and rode toward Violet Springs.

Before they reached the town they heard sporadic gunfire. Even as they reined up and sat motionless on their horses, eyes squinted against the rising sun, a rider came galloping toward them.

A hatless crow-faced man in a black suit, fancy gold vest, and string tie, he rode bent low in the saddle, whipping his horse with the reins and spurring it ever faster. But before he got more than fifty yards, rifle shots came from one of the outlying buildings, knocking him from the saddle. He landed sprawling, rolled over a few times, and lay dead in the dirt.

'Dammit, Mr Dunn, give me my gun,' Liberty demanded. 'Either that or consider yourselves accomplices to murder.'

Grudgingly, Bill pulled her Colt .45 from his belt and tossed it to her.

'I'll be holdin' you to your word, Deputy,' he warned. 'You shoot either one of us an' I swear to God not a Dunn will rest till you're feet up.'

'Don't worry,' she said. 'You may end up dead before we leave here, but it won't be my lead that caused it.'

Once the shooting stopped, Liberty and the Dunns kicked up their horses and rode toward town. Shortly, they passed the downed rider. Liberty reined up, dismounted, and made sure the cowboy was dead before climbing back into the saddle and continuing with the two brothers.

As they approached the outlying buildings three grim-faced gunmen stepped out from one of the shacks, rifles covering Liberty and the Dunns.

'Hold it right there,' the oldest of the three said. Then as they reined up: 'That fella lyin' out there — he kin to you?'

'Never seen him afore,' said Bill.

'He was a no-good cheatin' card-shark.'

'That settles it,' Bee said. 'Ain't no gamblers in our family, mister.'

The man studied them for another moment. Tall, gaunt and fierce-eyed with a stringy black beard, he resembled a Bible puncher as he intoned: 'Can thank the Almighty for that. A fella don't expect to win every hand, but losin' all the time gets mighty tiresome — 'specially when Satan's dealin' from the bottom of the deck.'

'Ain't that the truth?' Bee said, adding: 'Money's hard enough to come by these days without bein' cheated out of it.'

'Aye,' the man said. He eyed Liberty suspiciously. 'I know you from some place, sister?'

'Been to Guthrie or Clearwater lately?'

'Nope.'

'Then chances are you don't know me.'

The man didn't say anything. But he continued to stare at her.

Liberty nodded politely to him and nudged her buckskin on into town. The Dunn brothers followed, riding slowly but warily, each keeping his gun-hand near his holster.

Ahead, the rutted dirt street between the buildings was quiet and dappled by early sunlight. Liberty slowed her horse to a walk and looked about her. Two drunks were sleeping it off on the dirt sidewalk, and four saddled horses were tied up outside the Bottom Dollar. Two of the horses were bays with long black manes and tails. They'd been ridden hard recently and were caked with dried sweat. The other two, a blue roan and a chestnut, looked fresh. Liberty stored the description and condition of the horses away for possible future reference, and rode on toward the saloon. Lights were on inside and a large, muscular Negro in a shirt, threadbare pants, and bandage around his injured head stood emptying two brass spittoons in the street fronting the saloon.

'That there's Moses,' Bill told Liberty.

'Works for grub an' board.'

'Think he'd tell us where the McClorys are?'

'Not if he wants to see the sun come up tomorrow.'

Liberty thought a moment before saying: 'Since you've been here before, Mr Dunn, where do you think they'd be holed up?'

He stared at her in tight-lipped silence.

'You're right,' she said. 'Why should you help me if I can't help you collect the reward?'

Bill shrugged his bulky shoulders and spat his feelings into the dirt. 'Seems to me,' he drawled, 'there ain't no shame in accepting help when your life's on the line.'

'Don't suppose there is.'

'I mean, accepting and asking's two different things.'

'What're you driving at, Mr Dunn?'

'Well, I was thinking this way. If me 'n Bee just happened to be riding by when you jumped the McClorys — well, us knowing your pa an' all, we'd be *obliged* to make sure no one tried to gun you down from behind.'

'True,' Liberty said. 'And if that's the way it happened, then I'd feel *obliged* to thank you any way I could.'

'Including helpin' us collect the reward?' Bee said.

'Under the circumstances, what else could I do?'

'See,' Bill said to his brother, 'that's what schoolin' does for you. Makes sense out of no sense.'

Bee wasn't completely sold. As they got closer to the saloon, he eyed Liberty suspiciously. 'Just so there's no misunderstanding, Deputy, this ain't another one of them metalfores you mentioned earlier?'

'No,' Liberty said, suppressing a smile. 'What I'm suggesting is definitely not a metaphor. Now,' she added as the brothers looked relieved, 'would I be chasing my tail if I thought the McClorys were holed up in the Bottom Dollar?'

'Depends,' said Bill.

'On what?'

'Whether this young whore I hear Roy's sweet on is still spreadin' her legs for some gent up in her room or has called it quits and gone home.'

'This young whore — she have a name?'

'Ellie Rose.'

'And if 'Ellie' *had* called it quits,' Liberty said as they reined up outside the Bottom Dollar, 'would you happen to know where 'home' is?'

'Reckon I might,' Bill said soberly.

'Then we're all in accord,' Liberty said.

''Cord?'

'Agreement.'

'Ahh,' Bill said. 'Now there's a word you can shake hands with.'

Liberty rolled her eyes but didn't say anything. Dismounting, she tied her horse to the hitch-rail. 'Give me time to nose around, Mr Dunn, before you two show your hand.'

'Take all the time you want,' Bill said.

He took a cartridge from his gun-belt, inserted it into the empty chamber of his Colt, spun the cylinder, and re-holstered the gun. 'Just remember, Deputy — this ain't gonna be no church picnic like it was in Okfuskee Flats, when you fooled the Wallace brothers into letting you arrest 'em. This time nobody's gonna mistake you for some harmless, frilly-laced school teacher.'

Liberty looked at Bill in surprise. 'Is there anything you Dunns don't know about me?'

'I reckon not.'

'Be damned. Guess my days of sneaking up on outlaws are over.'

12

Moses finished emptying the spittoons and went to re-enter the saloon. As he did he saw Liberty approaching. Curious, he looked her over. Here was not only a woman dressed and armed with a six-gun like a man, but one that was both young and pretty as a wild flower — someone far different than the ugly, worn-out whores who inhabited Violet Springs.

Then he noticed it glinting on her shirt. Instantly, his curiosity turned to surprise and then disbelief as he realized she was a deputy US marshal.

'Stay right where you are,' Liberty ordered as he started for the door. 'I want to talk to you.'

He obeyed, a spittoon clutched in each big callused hand. ''Bout what?' he said. 'Ol' Mose ain't shot nobody. Ain't robbed nobody neither.'

'Then you're the only misfit in Hell Town who hasn't,' she said, adding: 'but right now your past doesn't interest me. All I want to know is if a certain whore named Ellie Rose is still upstairs?'

'Wouldn't know nothing 'bout no whores,' Moses said insolently — then stopped, mouth agape, eyes like saucers as he found himself looking into the muzzle of her Colt .45. He hadn't seen her jerk it, hadn't even seen her hand move and yet there it was — her six-gun aimed at his chest.

'Maybe you didn't hear me correctly,' Liberty said. 'So I'll ask you again. Is Ellie Rose upstairs or has she gone home?'

'She be upstairs, Marshal.'

'Sure about that?'

Moses nodded, 'Yes'm,' his gaze still riveted on the Colt in her hand.

'Thank you.' Liberty holstered her gun, as effortlessly as she'd drawn it, then stepped around the ex-slave and pushed through the batwing doors.

Moses stared after her, spittoons

forgotten, still amazed by how fast she had jerked her iron.

★ ★ ★

Inside, the Bottom Dollar was empty except for three people — the beautiful, well-dressed young man with the crystal-blue eyes and long yellow curls and his slender dark-eyed, dark-haired companion who were eating bacon and beans at a table at the rear; and the owner of the saloon, Cash Devlin, who stood at the register behind the bar. A tall, fleshy, balding man wearing metal-rimmed spectacles, he was busy totaling the night's receipts and on hearing someone enter, said without turning: 'Sorry, we're closed.'

'This won't take but a minute.'

Surprised to hear an educated female voice, Devlin turned and saw Liberty standing at the bar. His surprise faded as he saw the badge pinned on her chest, and with a knowing smile he said: 'Wondered when you'd show up, Marshal.'

'You were expecting me?' Liberty said, surprised.

'Been rumors.'

'That just *happened* to reach your ears?'

'Marshal, there ain't a rumor been born that didn't pass through Hell Town.'

'Then I guess I don't have to introduce myself.'

Devlin chuckled, tucked the bills he was holding into his pocket and closed the cash register drawer.

'Not when you're Marshal Macahan's protégé, no.' He reached under the bar, produced a dusty bottle of Four Roses bourbon, grabbed two glasses, and poured them both a generous drink.

'I insist,' he said when she shook her head. 'Last time I saw Ezra, I gave him my word that if I ever ran into you I'd buy you the best whiskey in the house.'

'Some other time,' Liberty said, ignoring the glass. 'Right now, all I want is information.'

'Ask away, Marshal. I'm a law-abiding fella — when there's any law to abide to.'

'It's Deputy, not Marshal. And I'm looking for the McClorys — '

'Ain't seen 'em — *Deputy*.'

'Might want to take a moment to think about it before you answer.'

'Don't have to. I ain't seen 'em. Period.'

'How about Ellie Rose? Think she'd know where they are?'

Devlin shrugged. 'Ask her yourself — she's upstairs.'

'Call her down,' Liberty ordered.

'Right now she's occupied.' His voice, like his eyes, hardened.

'With Roy McClory?'

Devlin smiled coldly. 'Reckon you didn't hear me straight — I ain't seen the McClorys.'

Liberty walked to the stairs leading up to the second floor. As she did she noticed the two young people finishing their meal at the rear of the saloon. Both had their backs to her and, deciding they represented no threat, she drew her Colt and fired a shot through the wooden ceiling. Upstairs, a woman shrieked.

The two young people at the table jumped, startled, and looked at Liberty. By then she'd turned her back on them and didn't see their faces. She walked under the next room and again fired up through the ceiling.

Another scream followed and this time a second floor door burst open and a fat young blonde, naked under a robe, whose cheaply-pretty face was sweaty and smeared with rouge, ran out. Leaning over the banisters, she yelled angrily at Devlin, demanding to know who was doing the shooting.

He turned to Liberty. 'Deputy, meet Miss Ellie Rose.'

'Get down here,' Liberty told her.

'Do I have to?' she asked Devlin.

'It's not up to him,' Liberty snapped. 'Now get down here!'

Grumbling, Ellie descended the stairs and confronted Liberty. 'What d'you want?'

'I'm looking for Roy McClory.'

'I ain't seen him. Him nor his cousin, neither.'

'I don't believe you,' Liberty said. 'I doubt if Judge Parker will either.'

Ellie looked uneasy. 'J-Judge Parker? Mean the Hanging Judge?'

'Yes. I'm taking you back to Guthrie.'

'You're arrestin' me?'

'That's right.'

'For what?'

'Harboring a known outlaw.'

'Doin' what?'

'Giving Roy McClory a place to hide.'

'That's a lie!'

'Not according to him. He bragged to his cellmate in Yuma Prison that you'd promised to let him hole up with you in Violet Springs.'

'That's another damn' lie!' spat Ellie. 'Jesus-on-a-cross, Marshal, you know how Roy is. He's the mother and father of all liars!'

'You'll get a chance to prove that in court. Now, turn around.' Liberty unhooked her wrist-irons from her belt and cuffed Ellie's hands behind her back.

'You just goin' to stand there and let her do this?' Ellie raged at Devlin.

'He has no choice,' Liberty said. 'Not unless he wants to buck the law and be arrested himself.'

Devlin eyed her grimly. 'Don't get on the prod with me, Deputy. You're a far piece from Guthrie an' there's lots of folks around here who'd pay admission to see a lawman dancing from a — ' He broke off as the Dunn brothers entered, both holding Winchesters and itching to use them.

'We heard shootin',' Bill said to Liberty. 'Wondered what was goin' on.'

'Mr Devlin, here,' she said pointedly, 'was about to persuade Ellie to tell me where Roy McClory is — isn't that *right*, Mr Devlin?'

Devlin glared at her, teeth gritted, then said to Ellie: 'You heard her. Start talking!'

Ellie hesitated, her watery blue eyes

filled with fear as she said: 'Roy will kill me if I do.'

'He'll have to kill me first,' Liberty said calmly. 'And I assure you that isn't likely. Now, where is he and, if you know, where's his cousin?'

'C-Could be they're at . . . my place.'

Liberty smiled. 'See, that wasn't so hard, was it? Now, go on upstairs and get dressed. You're going to take me to them.'

Ellie turned to Devlin. 'What about Ed Reece?'

'Tell him next time's on the house.'

Ellie nodded and plodded back upstairs.

'Go with her, Mr Dunn,' Liberty said to Bill. 'Make sure she doesn't have a sudden change of heart and climb out the window.'

★   ★   ★

Once Liberty, Ellie Rose and the Dunn brothers had left the Bottom Dollar, the two young people sitting in the rear of

100

the saloon pushed their empty plates away and sat back to finish their coffee.

'It don't make a lick of sense,' the dark-haired one said. 'You ride all over the territory looking for her just so you can ask her about Latigo and now, when she's right here in front of you, you don't say a word.'

'Timing wasn't right,' the blond-haired man said.

'The hell it wasn't.'

'Shhh, keep your voice down. I don't want anyone to hear us.'

His companion looked disgusted, removed her hat and impatiently pushed her bangs aside. 'When is it going to be right? Want to tell me that?'

'I can't,' said the man. 'I'll just know it when it is.'

'Well, I hope it's afore I get to be an old maid. 'Cause I got better things to do than traipse around the country after a lawman who once loved your — '

'No one's forcing you to traipse anywhere,' interrupted the man. 'It was your idea to follow me, not mine.'

'How we ever going to get hitched if I ain't with you? Or ain't gettin' hitched on your mind no more?'

''Course it's on my mind. I've told you that more than once already. But that doesn't mean we're getting married tomorrow or even next week. So either deal with it or walk. Your decision.' Rising, he added: 'Now, you coming or not?'

'Depends on where you're goin'.'

'Clearwater.'

'Why there?'

''Cause that's where Liberty's taking the McClorys.'

His companion scoffed. 'First she's gotta catch 'em, which ain't likely.' But she got up anyway and followed him out of the saloon.

13

Ellie Rose lived within walking distance of the Bottom Dollar. Escorted by Liberty and the Dunn brothers, she led them along a dirt path that climbed up a wooded slope behind the cemetery and ended in front of a rundown, sod-roofed shack.

Four unsaddled horses were tied to a line strung between two leafless trees growing near the shack. Liberty waited until she, Ellie, and the Dunns were a short distance from the front door, then stopped and told Bill and Bee to spread out, one on each side of her, and not to shoot until she gave the order. They obeyed without question.

Liberty levered a round into her rifle and told Ellie to walk ahead of her. Reluctantly and obviously frightened, Ellie obeyed. As they got closer they could hear men arguing inside the shack.

Suddenly the door opened and Travis McClory lurched out. He was drunk and after a couple of steps, stumbled and went sprawling. Raucous laughter followed him. A moment later two bearded men in trail-soiled clothes, with lined, weathered faces and the sun-squinted eyes of desert-riders, staggered out after him, followed by his older brother Roy.

All were as drunk as Travis and two of them, a brother-in-law, Sam Quincy and his nephew, Joe Blatty, were swigging from jugs of whiskey. Quincy drained his jug and went to toss it away when he saw Ellie and Liberty stopped a few paces in front of him.

He blinked, bleary-eyed, as if wondering if he was imagining them. Then, realizing he wasn't, he dropped the jug and went for his gun.

Liberty's right hand moved with blurring speed. Her Colt was out of her holster and pointed at his belly before his gun half-cleared leather.

'Sheathe it,' she told him. When he

grudgingly obeyed, she warned the others not to move.

The four men, including Travis, now on his knees, froze.

'Who in seven hells are you?' Roy snarled.

Liberty pulled her jacket back, revealing her badge. 'Deputy US Marshal — '

Before she could finish Ellie hurled herself at Liberty, catching her off-guard. Both women went sprawling, Liberty's gun flying from her hand.

With a drunken whoop Travis staggered to his feet, drew his six-gun, and aimed it unsteadily at Liberty.

As she stared up at him, death only an instant away, it dawned on her why the artist had drawn Travis McClory smiling on the Wanted poster. It was his signature before he killed anyone.

But this wasn't her time to die.

Before Travis could pull the trigger there was a rifle shot. The bullet tore a hole in his chest. He staggered back, eyes bugged, mouth agape, the gun dropping from his limp fingers as he collapsed on the dew-soaked earth.

Almost without pause a second rifle slug knocked the six-gun out of Quincy's hand. He jumped back, cursing, and grabbed his hand.

The Dunn brothers stepped out of the shadows, rifles leveled at the remaining men.

'I got your ride to hell right here,' Bill said, wagging his Winchester at them. 'So make your play, fellas.'

Eyes narrowed with hatred, the three men raised their hands.

Liberty picked up her Colt and told them to unbuckle their gun-belts.

Grudgingly, Roy and two his companions obeyed.

'S-Sorry, hon',' Ellie whined to Roy. 'I tried.'

He ignored her and glared at Bill. 'You tit-suckin' yellow dog,' he hissed. 'My whole family will track you down and make sure you die real slow for this.'

'They won't have to go far,' Bill said. ''Cause soon as your feet are kickin' air, me 'n my brothers will be huntin' them. And that's a plain fact!'

Once the three outlaws were securely roped to their horses, Liberty had the Dunn brothers wrap Travis' body in a blanket and tie the corpse over his saddle.

'What about me, Marshal?' Ellie asked. 'You still plan on takin' me back to Guthrie?'

'Break the law, pay the price,' Liberty said, adding: 'dammit, girl, if things had worked out the way you planned, I'd be dead by now.'

'I know,' Ellie admitted. 'Love can make an awful fool out of you.'

'Love,' scoffed Bill. 'Closest you been to love is countin' the dollars you made by spreadin' your legs.'

'Those are harsh words coming from the likes of you,' Ellie said, stung. 'I mean, you ain't no stranger to what I'm selling.'

'Maybe not, girl. Difference is, and it's a mighty big difference, I don't confuse whorin' with love.' Turning to

Liberty, Bill added: 'We got what we came for. Time we cashed in our chips.'

Liberty hesitated, torn. Remembering how much she'd loved Latigo Rawlins and knowing that she would have gone against her father's wishes and married the Texas gunman if he'd lived, she felt a pang of empathy.

'You got folks, Ellie Rose?'

'Sure. Back in Ohio.'

'If I don't arrest you, will you give up whoring and go home?'

Ellie's pale blue eyes brightened. 'You mean that for true?'

'Home or jail — your choice.'

Ellie looked at Roy, tied astride his horse, then back at Liberty.

'That's easy, Marshal. I'll go home.'

'Then get inside, pack your stuff and don't let me ever see your face in the Territory again — because if I do, I'll arrest you on the spot. Clear?'

'Y-Yes, an' — an' thank you, Marshal. You won't regret it. Promise.' Ellie hurried into the shack.

'You a damn fool, Deputy.' Bill spat

disgustedly. 'Lettin' your heart rule your head over a no-good whore.'

'Maybe a second chance will straighten her out,' Liberty said.

Bill snorted. 'You think Ezra would've given that lyin' little bitch a second chance?'

'I've no idea what he would have done,' Liberty retorted. 'Much as I admire and respect Marshal Macahan, I'm not him. Nor would he want me to be. I'm my own person. And so long as I'm wearing this badge, I'll do as I see fit. And what fits is giving Ellie another chance. Now,' she added, stepping up into the saddle, 'let's quit yammering at each other and get started for Clearwater.'

'And then what?' demanded Bee.

'I'll make out the necessary paperwork entitling you to the reward and then tomorrow morning, take my prisoners to Guthrie. Sound satisfactory?'

'Reckon,' Bill said.

'Then let's make dust.'

14

It was late afternoon when they finally rode into Clearwater. The normal midday hustle and bustle had died down, but there were still plenty of people about and enough riders, wagons, and buckboards to fill the hot, windless air with dust.

Liberty, grateful to have made the long ride from Violet Springs without incident, led her prisoners and the Dunn brothers along Main Street toward the sheriff's office.

People on the boardwalks stopped and watched as Liberty and the others rode past, their expressions a mixture of curiosity and concern as they saw the blanket-wrapped corpse draped face-down on the back of one of the horses.

Two of the people watching were the blond man and his companion. Standing by their horses, which were tied up outside Jan's Café, they'd shed their dusters revealing they were dressed as differently as they looked. The slender, dark-eyed woman wore a plaid shirt that had leather elbow patches on each sleeve, frayed jeans and knee-high Apache moccasins; while the handsome young man was dressed as stylishly as a riverboat gambler.

In the middle of the street a bunch of children raced ahead of Liberty. Excited by a dead outlaw's body as only youngsters can be, they shouted her name aloud to everyone. Their voices were shrill and by the time she reined up outside the sun-and-shadow-dappled sheriff's office, Will Hagen was already standing there, leaned against the hitching rail, awaiting her.

His usual smug look was replaced by an angry scowl. Annoyed by her success, he waited until Liberty had dismounted and told the Dunn brothers to help the prisoners off their horses, then he confronted her.

'Hope you ain't expectin' to leave

your prisoners in jail overnight, Deputy.'

'Where the hell else would I leave them?'

'That ain't my problem. But, in case you've forgotten, all the bars are being replaced and right now there's nothin' but empty space to stop a prisoner from escaping from both cells.'

Liberty looked at him incredulously. 'You can't be serious?'

'Ah, but I am.'

'But we already discussed this with the mayor, Will — last week if you remember — and it was decided that you'd do one cell at a time so that we'd have somewhere to keep anyone who was arrested.'

He smirked. 'I know that, Deputy, but right after that meeting I talked to the mayor again and he agreed with me that it would save time and money if we did both cells at once.'

Liberty wanted to hit him. Instead, remembering Marshal Macahan's soothing *'Caution's the way'* she fought down her temper and said quietly: 'Why wasn't

I informed of your new plans?'

'Most likely, 'cause you were in Guthrie,' he said smugly.

'Dammit, isn't that what the telegraph's for?'

'Indeed. But I've been busy.' Before she could say anything, he added sarcastically: 'And important as the marshal's office is, Deputy, you can't expect me to drop everything in order to keep you posted on every bit of news as it happens.'

Liberty, realizing that he was goading her, again kept her temper and said only: 'Well, bars or no bars, I'll be keeping my prisoners here until the morning train to Guthrie arrives. So warn your deputy to yell out before he enters the office after dinner. Otherwise, he'll be eating a load of double-ought buckshot for dessert.' Before the sheriff could protest, she turned to the Dunns, adding: 'If you're still interested in that reward money, I'll need you to take turns guarding the prisoners with me tonight.'

'Be happy to, Deputy,' Bill said. 'Me 'n' Bee, we're always willin' to oblige a Federal officer.'

'Now wait a damn minute,' began Sheriff Hagen. 'These boys ain't been legally deputized — '

'Sure they have,' Liberty said sweetly. 'I swore them in just before we left Violet Springs. Isn't that right?' she said to the Dunns.

Both nodded. 'All we need is badges,' Bill said wryly.

'I'm sure Sheriff Hagen has plenty of extras in his desk drawer,' Liberty said; then turning her back on the glowering lawman, she looked at her prisoners and thumbed at the office. 'Inside if you please, gentlemen.'

Grimly but without any protest, the three outlaws obeyed.

There were two adjoining cells in the jail attached to the sheriff's office, each with two bunks in them: Liberty had the Dunns drag one of the bunks from the first cell into the end cell, then herded the prisoners into the cell and tied her rope across the empty space where the bars had once been.

'Stay on your bunks,' she warned the outlaws. 'Any of you comes even near that rope, I'm going to pretend you're trying to escape and shoot you. We clear on that?'

15

Evening became night and the night dragged slowly by.

Liberty took the first shift guarding the prisoners, while the Dunn brothers ate supper in the Silver Spur across the street from the sheriff's office. Determined not to fall asleep, she deliberately sat on a hard-backed chair in the jail, Winchester across her lap, drinking black coffee as she kept watch on the three outlaws stretched out on their bunks. They all wore leg-irons that clanked whenever they moved and each man had been fed a ham sandwich and a mug of coffee brought in from Jan's Café.

None of them had said much since they'd been jailed. Quincy and Blatty occasionally exchanged a few muttered words, but Roy McClory remained grimly quiet. He lay there staring up at the ceiling, smoking one hand-rolled after another, eyes hidden from Liberty by the brim of his pulled-down hat, his raspy breathing the only sound coming from him.

Watching him, Liberty felt a sense of lurking danger — the same kind of danger she'd once felt while watching a rattler, coiled and ready to strike.

My God, she thought, fighting not to yawn, *I'll be damned glad to get these men to Guthrie and turn them over to the jailor.*

A noise outside interrupted her thinking. Rising, she skirted the rope enclosing the outlaws and entered the first cell. There she paused and looked at the prisoners, making sure none of them had moved, then stood on the remaining bunk and peered out the unbarred window.

The unlighted alley behind the jail appeared to be empty. She leaned her head out far enough to see in both directions but saw no one. Blaming the noise on a stray cat, she went to pull her head in — when she heard a faint whirling sound.

It was one of those sounds that was both familiar and yet unfamiliar — and it took a moment for her to realize what it was. By then it was too late.

A rope snaked out of the darkness, the noose looping around her neck. Startled, she tried to pull it over her head. Before she could, or even cry out, the noose was pulled tight, choking off any sound.

Gasping for breath, she felt herself dragged out through the window. She tried to resist but the force pulling her was too strong and she landed hard on the dirt. Winded, she felt herself being pulled along. She tried to see who her captors were. But she couldn't turn her head enough and all she caught was a glimpse of several shadowy riders with spare horses beyond the corral fence on the other side of the alley.

The rope was attached to the saddlehorn of one of the riders. His horse was backing up and Liberty was dragged toward the fence. Choked by the rope, her senses unclear, she could offer little resistance.

Meanwhile, above her, Roy and the other outlaws came wriggling out of the two unbarred windows. Jumping down, they quickly joined the riders who'd ridden out the corral and were now grouped around Liberty.

'Want us to stretch her neck?' a young rider named Seth asked Roy.

'Nah. Hanging's too good for the bitch.' He hunkered down beside Liberty and loosened the rope around her neck. Barely conscious, she gasped for air, too weak and dazed to even sit up. Roy leered at her. 'Should've killed me, Deputy, when you had the chance.'

Liberty tried to speak but only strangled gasps came out.

'She the one who shot my nephew?' asked another rider. He was short and mean-eyed like Roy, but older, heavier and gray-haired.

'Uh-uh, that was them bastards, the Dunns,' Roy said. 'But she's just as responsible, Uncle Drew, 'cause without her offering them reward money, they most likely wouldn't have been so quick to pull the trigger.'

'Where're the Dunns now?' Drew asked.

'Eatin' supper in the saloon 'cross the street,' said Quincy.

One of the other riders, Cal Dugan, nudged his horse closer, saying: 'What do you say we make it their last supper?'

'You're readin' my mind, cousin.' Roy grabbed the rope still around Liberty's neck, and motioned to the rider to untie it from his saddlehorn. Then, jerking her to her feet, said: 'Wouldn't want you to miss this, Deputy.' He pulled her along, the rope choking off her protests.

16

At that time of night all the stores were closed and Main Street was deserted save for two cowboys leaving the Silver Spur. Roy, watching from the alley opposite, waited until they'd mounted and ridden off before telling his men to follow him. He then dragged Liberty across the street to the saloon where he paused and peered in through the window.

Inside, the saloon was crowded and noisy. Men were lined along the bar while others played poker at the tables in back. Roy looked for the Dunn brothers and finally spotted them seated in a corner drinking a beer after their meal. A hard-faced, redheaded waitress said something that made them laugh as she cleared away their dirty plates, and Bee jokingly pinched her on the butt as she walked off.

Roy turned to one of his cousins. 'Stay with the horses,' he told him. Then to his uncles and other relatives: 'Rest of you, come with me.'

As he was talking, Liberty noticed his hold on the rope had slackened. And before anyone realized, she spun around so that her back was to the window and hurled herself backward through the glass.

Everyone in the saloon whirled around as the window shattered and broken glass flew everywhere.

Unhurt, Liberty rolled over and jumped to her feet, at the same time pulling the rope so hard Roy was almost jerked off balance. He staggered forward and in order to save himself from falling into the remaining jagged glass, dropped the rope and braced himself against the frame of the window.

Inside the saloon Liberty threw off the noose, and elbowed her way through the startled crowd to the bar. Ducking behind it, she grabbed the sawed-off shotgun that the barkeep kept hidden under the bar for protection. Breaking it open, she made sure the scattergun was loaded then straightened up and aimed it at the McClory clan gathered outside the broken window.

'You got five seconds to throw your guns down,' she yelled. 'One, two, three — '

She got no further.

Roy jumped back from the window, snatched the six-gun tucked in his belt, and started firing at her.

Liberty pulled both triggers. The roar was deafening as a double load of buckshot blasted away the remaining glass, along with most of the frame, killing Blatty, who happened to be closest to the window.

Immediately Quincy and the McClorys scattered and ran for cover. Within moments they were positioned behind rain barrels, water troughs, fences, posts and anything else they could find to hide behind and were pouring lead in through the windows and under the batwings doors.

Everyone in the saloon hit the floor,

bullets zipping about their heads.

Liberty swapped her shotgun for a rifle belonging to a nearby man who, in his hurry to take cover, had left it leaned against the bar. Pumping in a round, she ran to the window. Keeping hidden behind the wall, she fired at the first man she saw — which was Roy's uncle, Drew. She missed him but chipped wood out of a fence post inches from his head, making him curse and duck back out of sight.

Liberty, realizing she was an easy target in the saloon lights, yelled to the barkeep to turn them off. Before he could obey her, a bullet shattered the mirror behind the bar. Shards of broken glass shattered on the floor, while other bullets peppered the walls and tables and rows of bottles lined on either side of the mirror.

Someone crawled up beside Liberty. She saw it was Bill Dunn and his brother Bee.

'How the hell did them bastards break out?' Bill demanded.

'Yeah,' added Bee, 'what happened, Deputy, you fall asleep?'

'Shut up and shoot!' she barked.

Grumbling, they obeyed, taking up positions on either side of the entrance and firing at the outlaws from under the batwing doors.

The gunfight lasted nonstop for several minutes. Then during a lull, shots were fired by someone farther up the street. One of the McClory clan pitched forward, dead. More firing followed and the McClorys, realizing they were caught in a deadly crossfire, stopped shooting and ran to their horses in the alley beside the sheriff's office.

'What the devil . . . ?' Liberty began. Cautiously leaning her head out the broken window, she looked in both directions. To her right she saw two people crouched behind an empty freight wagon parked outside Kinsley Mercantile. Without a moon or street lights it was too dark to see their faces, just their hats and rifles, and she wondered who they were. Waiting until the McClory clan had ridden off, she told the Dunn brothers to keep her covered then stepped outside.

Once on the boardwalk, she signaled to the people behind the wagon to show themselves.

They obeyed, rifles lowered, and slowly walked toward her. Liberty didn't recognize them until they got closer — then she realized it was the two young people she'd seen eating in the Bottom Dollar.

Surprised, she studied them as they drew near. There was something very familiar about both of them. But it was only when they stepped on to the boardwalk and the light from the saloon revealed their faces that she realized the blond-haired man resembled Latigo Rawlins — making her heart jump. At the same time she realized the one with dark hair looked vaguely like —

'Raven?' she exclaimed. 'Raven Bjorkman, is that you?'

'Yes'm,' Raven replied. 'Been a fair spell since I last seen you.'

'More years than I care to count,'
Liberty said. 'And you,' she added to
the blond-haired man, 'you're a dead
ringer for — '

'My older brother, yes, I know.'

'Y-You're Latigo Rawlins' kid brother?'

'Yes, ma'am.'

'Of course you are,' she said. 'My
God, you're like two peas in a pod.' She
stuck out her hand. 'I'm Liberty Mercer.'

'Latt,' he said, shaking hands. 'Sure
glad I finally caught up with you,
ma'am.'

''Ma'am?'' She laughed. 'Hell, we're
too close to the same age for you to be
calling me ma'am. Same goes for you,'
she said to Raven. 'So let's forget about
formality, all right, and call each other
by our first names?'

'Suits me,' Raven said.

'Me, too,' agreed Latt. He studied
Liberty questioningly before saying: 'I
don't mean to be nosy, but when my
brother knew you, weren't you called
Emily?'

'Emily Margaret Mercer, yes,' she

127

said, adding: 'How'd you know that? Did Latigo tell you?'

'Uh-huh. That's one of the reasons it took a while to catch up with you — I didn't tie the two names together.'

'Yeah, I guess it is confusing. Oh, before I forget,' she went on, 'thanks for throwing in with me. It turned the fight around.'

Latt shrugged, as if it was nothing. 'You'll be riding after them, I reckon?'

'Come daylight, sure.'

'Then we got to talk tonight.'

'About your brother, you mean? I'm sorry. Much as I'd like to hear all you've got to say, it'll have to keep. I — '

'This isn't about Latigo.'

'What, then?'

Latt looked at the Dunn brothers, who were standing in the saloon doorway behind Liberty, and said: 'No disrespect, gents, but what I've got to say is for the deputy's ears only.'

Liberty turned to Bill. 'Could you two round up the mortician for me and ask him to take care of the bodies? Oh, and tell him the law will pay for the coffins.'

'Sure thing, Deputy. But after that, you're on your own. Me 'n Bee, here, we've already done enough to earn that reward.'

'More than enough,' Liberty agreed. 'Only problem is, the only money you're entitled to is for Travis.'

'How d'you mean?'

'You saw; Roy and Quincy escaped.'

'That ain't our fault,' Bee said angrily. 'We helped you capture 'em, and we sure enough helped you put 'em in jail. Just 'cause you were fool enough to let the bastards escape, hell, that ain't our fault.'

'Damn right it ain't,' Bill said. 'We done our job and we earned that there reward.'

'I agree with you,' Liberty said. 'But the marshal's office doesn't see it that way. No prisoners, no reward. Simple as that.'

The Dunn brothers glared at her.

Bee's gun hand inched toward the Colt holstered on his hip.

'Don't even think of it,' Liberty warned him. 'Or there'll be another corpse lying in the street and it won't be mine.'

Bill slapped his brother's gun hand aside. 'Don't be an idiot,' he said and then pushed him toward the entrance to the saloon. 'Go buy us a bottle. I'll join you soon as I get through talkin' to the deputy, here. You heard me,' he added when Bee didn't move. 'Get in there.'

Grudgingly, Bee pushed in through the batwing doors.

Bill turned back to Liberty. 'From now on, Deputy, you got yourself two extra shadows.'

'I'll be sure to watch my back.'

'Didn't mean it like that.'

'Then how did you mean it?'

'Just that me 'n my brother aim on gettin' all that reward — even if it means doggin' your trail for as long as it takes to round up Roy and Quincy again.'

'That won't be necessary,' Liberty assured him. 'Travis is already dead and you'll be paid for that. Then when I get Roy and Quincy behind bars again, with or without you, I'll honor my word and see to it that you get the rest of the reward.'

Bill studied her for a long moment. 'I believe you,' he said. 'But we'll still tag along, Deputy, 'case it should just happen to slip your mind.' Turning, he entered the saloon before she could argue.

Liberty turned back to Latt and Raven. 'C'mon,' she told them. 'Let's go to my house. It's the only place I know in Clearwater where the walls don't have ears.'

17

The small wood-frame house was set back among a stand of pink and white dogwood trees at the edge of town. Liberty had lived there ever since she'd been transferred from Guthrie to Clearwater. It wasn't much of a house, and the furniture that came with it was old and in shabby condition, but Liberty had tried to cheer things up by repainting the bedroom, hanging new curtains in the living area, and filling vases with fragrant wild flowers that grew near the trees.

Now, as she lit the hurricane lamp and set it on the table, she offered to make Latt and Raven a fresh pot of coffee.

'Let me do it,' Raven said, going to the iron stove by the window. 'You two go ahead and talk.'

Thanking her, Liberty pointed at a cupboard. 'You'll find beans and the grinder in there on the top shelf. Now,' she added, sitting across the table from Latt, 'what's so important that can't wait till tomorrow?'

Latt took an envelope out of his saddle-bag, pulled a sepia photograph from it, and handed it to Liberty. 'First, take a look at this.'

Liberty obeyed, and realized she was looking at a young blond woman of around twenty who greatly resembled Latigo and Latt.

'Her name's Rainy,' Latt said. 'She's my kid sister.'

Liberty frowned, surprised. 'I didn't know Latigo had a sister. Or a brother, either, for that matter.'

Now it was Latt's turn to be surprised. 'He never mentioned us?'

'Not that I can remember, no. He and I were very close, but there was a lot going on then and not much time to talk about our pasts.'

'I reckon not.'

'Guess we always figured that we had the rest of our lives together to fill in the blanks, so to speak. But Fate cut that short . . . ' Pausing, Liberty looked at the photo again, then said: 'Rainy — that's an unusual name.'

'It was raining buckets the day she was born,' Latt explained, 'so instead of calling her Ellen, like Ma had planned, she decided to call her Rainy, after the rainy day. Kind of loco when you think about it, but . . . ' His voice trailed off.

Liberty studied the photo. 'She's very pretty. Where is she now?'

'The McClorys got her,' said Raven as she brought the coffee pot and three mugs to the table.

'McClorys?' Liberty echoed.

Latt nodded grimly. 'They kidnapped her about a month ago — well, Seth, the youngest did — and took her to their hideout in the Seminole Nation.'

'It's in the badlands, not far from Violet Springs,' put in Raven.

'I know it,' Liberty said. 'Last I heard the whole clan was holed up in Silver Rock Canyon, near an old played-out mine.'

'They're still there,' Latt said. 'We tracked them — '

'*I* tracked them,' corrected Raven. 'You couldn't follow a blind steer if it was walkin' in mud.'

' — all the way to the mouth of the canyon,' Latt continued, unfazed by Raven's sarcasm. 'But when we saw how many of them there were, we decided to get help.'

'Smart move,' Liberty said. Then: 'Did you actually see your sister with them?'

'No. But she's there all right.'

'How do you know?'

'We were with her when Seth rode off with her,' Raven said.

'I was with her,' Latt corrected. 'You were off huntin' supper.'

'Well, someone had to kill somethin' for the pot. If I'd left it up to you, we would've starved — '

'All right, that's enough! Quit bickering,' Liberty said. Then to Latt: 'Why'd you pick me for this? You could've gone to any marshal.'

''Any' marshal wasn't in love with my brother. And because of the way you felt about him, and the fact that you have a reputation for never quitting, I knew I couldn't do any better.'

Liberty felt good inside. Someone finally believed in her enough to overlook the fact that she was a woman.

'Will you help us?' Latt asked. 'I mean, you're going after the McClorys anyway, so it ain't like we're dragging you away from anything important.'

'And I'll track for you,' Raven said.

Liberty frowned, dubious.

'Raven's short on discipline,' Latt said quickly, 'but she can track man or animal over any terrain — even bare rocks if need be.'

'How'd you learn to do that?' Liberty asked Raven. 'Last I recall you were living on a little spread with your mother outside Santa Rosa.'

'Still would be, most likely,' Raven said, 'if Latt hadn't stopped by our place one day to water his horse.'

'And to ask you about what you

remembered about my brother.'

'As for your question, Deputy,' Raven continued, 'I learned about tracking from the Mescaleros. My folks were right friendly with them and after Pa was killed, I spent a lot of time on their reservation — '

'Wait a minute,' Liberty broke in. 'Wasn't it the Mescaleros who once saved Gabriel Moonlight's life?'

Raven nodded. 'I found him shot to pieces in the desert and fetched him home. Ma had me ride to the reservation and ask the medicine man, Almighty Sky, for help. He wasn't happy about it, but 'cause it was Ma he brung along their sacred healer, Lolotea, a young blind girl with long white hair who wasn't supposed to ever leave the reservation. She spent the night in our barn with Gabe, and by morning, he was healed.'

'Is that another of your tall tales,' Latt asked Raven, 'or did it really happen that way?'

Raven dismissed him with a disdainful look then turned to Liberty, saying:

'You were friends with Gabe, weren't you?'

'Yes. He rode with me. And also with your brother,' she said to Latt. 'In fact they . . . ' She broke off uncomfortably.

' — were killed together in Mexico,' he finished. 'Yes, I know.'

'Sorry. I didn't mean to bring that up.'

'It's all right,' he said. 'I barely knew Latigo. And what little I did know 'bout him — and all the men he killed, most of 'em without much provocation — is one of the reasons I want to be a lawman. I want to try and restore some dignity to the family name.' He sipped his coffee and smiled at Raven. 'You sure make good coffee, girl.'

'I ain't no girl,' Raven said fiercely. 'I'm a full-growed woman and I'll have you remember that, Mr Latham Rawlins.'

'Latham?' Liberty frowned. 'Thought you said your name was Latt?'

'It is — '

'He shortened it to Latt,' Raven said,

laughing, "'cause he thought Latham sounded too pretty . . . too fancy.'

'That's a damned lie!'

'Bein' so pretty and fancy himself,' she continued, 'he figured he ought to have a more meat-an'-potatoes name. You know. Somethin' that sounded more . . . manly.'

'Don't listen to her,' Latt told Liberty. 'I swear she's lying.'

'Why would I lie 'bout that?' Raven said. 'I mean, shoot, I didn't even know you then.' She laughed again, knowing by Latt's scowl that she'd successfully tweaked his tail.

'You'd better cut it out,' he warned, 'or you're going to regret it.'

Raven winked at Liberty. 'Swears he's going put me over his knee and swat the daylights out of me. 'Course he knows better than to try. I'd just wait till he was asleep and then carve my initials on his chest.'

Latt started to respond but Liberty cut him off and glowered at both of them. 'I told you two to quit bickering.'

'Sorry.'

'So, will you help us?'

Liberty sighed. 'All right. I'll try to get your sister back — on two conditions.'

'Name them.'

'That it doesn't interfere with my rounding up Roy McClory or Sam Quincy or any of the other McClorys who deserve to be arrested.'

'What else?'

'I call the shots. This has to be done legally. You OK with that?'

Latt nodded.

'What about you?' Liberty asked Raven. 'You willing to do what I tell you?'

'Reckon so.'

'Yes or no?'

'Yes.'

'Then raise your right hands, both of you,' Liberty said, 'and I'll swear you in.'

18

The next morning after breakfast, the three of them collected their horses from the livery and rode to the train station. They were followed by the Dunn brothers, who made no effort to hide themselves.

'Looks like we got company,' Latt said as he saw Bill and Bee riding a short distance behind them.

Liberty nodded, made a quick decision and reined up. 'Guess you were serious about being my shadows,' she said when the Dunns caught up with her.

'Serious as serious can be,' Bill said.

'Then know this: if you ride with me, you have to be sworn in as deputies.'

'I thought we was already sworn in,' Bee said. 'Least, that's what you told Sheriff Hagen.'

'That was just for show and you

know it,' Liberty said. 'This time's different. It has to be official and you and your brother have to follow my orders same as Latt and Raven here. You boys willing to do that?'

Bill looked at her incredulously. 'You'd actually make us *deputies*?'

Liberty laughed sourly. 'Ironic, I know, considering how you Dunn boys play loose and easy with the law. But under the circumstances, yes, I'd have to. Now, do we have a deal?'

'What about the reward? Do we got to share it with them?' Bill said, thumbing at Latt and Raven.

'No,' Liberty replied. 'They're helping me for an entirely different reason. Besides, like I told you yesterday, soon as Roy and Quincy are under lock and key again, the rest of the reward's yours. Got my word on it.'

'Then it's a deal,' Bill said. 'Swear away, Deputy.'

★　★　★

The morning train to Clearwater was an hour late. When it finally chugged into the station, the conductor, in order to make up for lost time, told Liberty and the others to load their horses as quickly as possible.

'You go first,' Liberty told Raven, Latt, and the Dunns. 'Regret's not likely to enter that car without a fuss, and I don't want to rile up your horses before you get them loaded.'

Watched impatiently by the engineer and the conductor Latt, Raven, and the Dunns led their horses up the ramp into the boxcar, unsaddled them, and quickly put them in their stalls. It only took a few minutes. But when Liberty led Regret to the ramp, the irascible buckskin shied away and tried to bite her. Not wasting any time, she took off her denim jacket and tied it over the stallion's head. Unable to see, Regret settled down and allowed Liberty to lead it up the ramp and into its stall.

The five of them then took their seats aboard the train and settled in for the ride to Clearwater. The Dunns sat across the aisle from Liberty, pulled their trail-soiled hats down over their eyes, and soon fell asleep.

Liberty, who sat facing Latt and Raven, opened one of her saddle-bags, took out a wrapped bundle and handed it to Latt, saying: 'I've been holding on to these for personal reasons. Now I want you to have them.'

Curious, Latt opened the bundle to reveal a black gun-belt with two ivory-grip, nickel-plated Colt .44s tucked into well-oiled, tie-down holsters. He studied them, speechless, and then looked at Liberty in disbelief.

'A-Are these my brother's?'

She nodded. 'I brought them home with me after he died.'

'My God,' he breathed. 'After all these years . . . '

'They must mean a lot to you, Deputy,' Raven said.

Liberty nodded.

'Then maybe you should keep them?' Latt said.

'No. Rightfully, they're yours.' She paused and shook her head as if she couldn't believe her thoughts. 'It's hard to believe now, but I once loved your brother enough to consider running off with him.'

'Gabe Moonlight told Momma that you two planned to get hitched,' Raven said. 'That true?'

Liberty nodded. 'It was right after I left St Mark's. I was only fifteen or sixteen, and I couldn't imagine life without him.' She shook her head, said ruefully: ''Course, Drifter — my dad — wasn't too happy about the idea. Tried to make me understand what a big mistake it would be. But I was too headstrong and too young to know better, so naturally I wouldn't listen.' She sighed, troubled, before adding: 'That was a lifetime ago. I've moved on since then.'

'But won't these guns help keep his memory alive for you?'

'I don't need anything to keep his memory alive. All I have to do is close my eyes and it all comes back to me like it was yesterday.'

'Then I'll gladly take them,' Latt said, admiring the matching Colts. 'Maybe even swap them for mine.'

Raven frowned. 'I wouldn't do that. Your brother killed a lot of folks with those guns. They're probably cursed or somethin' and will bring you bad luck.'

Latt laughed. 'That's ridiculous. Guns can't be cursed. They can't bring people bad luck either — any more than a hammer or a saw can.'

'I hope you're right,' Raven said, unconvinced. 'But if I was you, I'd still get rid of them.'

'Well, you're not me. So quit working up a sweat over something that ain't none of your business.'

Raven made a face. 'Fine. But if you get shot while we're trying to rescue your sister, don't blame me, 'cause I warned you.' She turned to Liberty. 'I'll be back in a minute.'

'Where you going?'

'To find the conductor and ask him

to tell the engineer to let us off at Valley Verde. It's much closer to Momma's grave than Santa Rosa — if that's OK with you, Deputy?'

Ignoring Raven's sarcastic tone, Liberty nodded.

Raven hurried off.

'She ain't the sweetest berry on the bush,' Latt said wryly, 'but once you get past her orneriness and natural distrust of the law, you'll find she's well worth her salt.'

Liberty chuckled. 'Then she should fit right in with the rest of us misfits.'

19

Valley Verde occupied the center of a deep volcanic basin that was sheltered on three sides by steep, flat-topped cliffs shaped like a horseshoe. Shaded from the relentless New Mexico sun by the towering cliffs, the valley was green and peaceful, with a creek running through the south end, and was home to wild horses, coyotes, rattlers, and various other forms of wildlife.

The railroad tracks ran along the southern edge of the basin, following an old winding wagon trail that, due to the railroad, was now extinct.

Dark clouds hid the moon when the engineer stopped the train by a rocky outcrop alongside the trail. There was no station and it wasn't an official stop, but it was a known fact that if warned ahead of time the conductor allowed people who lived on the outskirts of town to get off. Tonight was no exception. But it was so dark he needed his lantern to unlock the boxcar. Sliding the door aside, he dragged out the wooden ramp and clamped it into position.

Liberty and the others, who'd already jumped down, quickly unloaded their horses from the boxcar. Expecting trouble from Regret, Liberty took off her jacket to blindfold him. But the unpredictable buckskin meekly allowed her to lead him from his stall, saddle him, and walk him down the ramp without the slightest resistance.

'How come he's so docile all of a sudden?' Raven said. 'Is he afraid of the dark?' As she spoke she approached the buckskin and reached out to pet him.

'No — don't!' exclaimed Liberty.

She was too late. Regret took a vicious swipe at Raven, and only Bee Dunn's quick reflexes saved her from an ugly bite. Even so, as he pulled her aside, the buckskin's big yellow teeth clamped on the sleeve of her doeskin jacket, ripping the leather and nipping Raven's wrist.

'Good-God-awmighty!' she yelped.

'I warned you he was bad-tempered,' Liberty said. 'But for Bee, here, you might be nursing a broken wrist.'

Raven nodded, grateful. 'Thanks,' she said to Bee. 'I'm in your debt, Mr Dunn.'

'More'n welcome,' Bee said shyly, and moved off to join his brother.

Raven glared at the buckskin and grumbled: 'Sonofabitch is lucky I don't shoot him.'

Liberty chuckled. 'You'd have to stand at the end of a very long line.' Stepping up into the saddle, she waited for the others to mount and then the five of them rode off in the direction of the Bjorkman ranch.

★   ★   ★

After they'd ridden a mile or so, the moon appeared from behind the clouds. Its pale silvery light showed they were riding across a flat, arid valley sheltered on the north and east by mountains. A range of distant lumpy hills could be seen to the west; while the south lay open all the way to Mexico, which was farther than they could see. Ahead, big craggy outcrops of rock loomed up like dark sentinels guarding the wasteland.

As they rode, Liberty asked Raven if she ever regretted the fact that her mother had sold the ranch instead of leaving it to her. Raven shrugged and said that she'd often wondered how it would have felt living alone in the cabin where she'd been born, but finally decided that it would have been like living with a ghost. Two ghosts in fact, because even after all these years, it was hard for her to admit that her father was dead. 'What about you?' she asked Liberty. 'Would you sell your spread if your pa died?'

'I think so, yes — ' Liberty paused as a bleached white steer skull in the trail made the buckskin shy, almost unseating her, and then said: 'I don't think I could stay in the house, with all the memories of my father facing me every time I turned around. I'd sooner start afresh someplace else.'

'I feel the same way,' Raven said. ''Course,' she added grimly, 'it might've been different if old man Stadtlander weren't still alive, since he's the one who's responsible for all my grief.'

'I thought you said it was his son, Slade, who shot your pa,' said Latt. 'And he's dead.'

'Don't matter,' Raven said. 'Stadtlander spawned Slade and made him what he was, and I'll never quit hating that old bastard till he's feet up.'

'From what I hear, you won't have to wait much longer,' Liberty said. 'Between his arthritis, gout, and heart problems, seems like he's not long for this world.'

'Another minute's too long for me,' Raven said bitterly. As if not wanting to talk any longer, she kicked up her horse and rode ahead of them.

'She's one strange girl,' Latt said. 'Just when I think I got her all figured out, she says or does something that makes me realize I don't know her at all.' He sighed. 'Sometimes I can't believe that I actually love her and am thinking of asking her to marry me.'

'Love's like that,' Liberty said. 'It doesn't play by any rules. It's hit or miss at best. And it takes all types to make it work.'

'You mean like you and Latigo?'

'I went straight from a convent into the arms of a deadly gunman and bounty hunter. You can't find two more different types than that.'

'Then you really would have married him?'

'That's what I kept telling myself, yes. 'Course, I had a very school-girlish, romantic vision of him back then. Later, after he gunned down my namesake in Mexico, I began to wonder a little — you know, whether Drifter wasn't right about him; that maybe Latigo really was a heartless killer after all, and that marrying him would be a huge, life-altering mistake.'

Latt didn't answer. They rode on in silence.

Liberty thought they'd finished talking, but after a few minutes he said wistfully: 'No matter what he was, or did, I wish I'd known him better.'

'Maybe I can help you there,' Liberty said. 'I'll be happy to answer any questions you may have about him.'

'I'd appreciate that, Deputy. Truth is, deep down that's probably another reason why I wanted to find you. So I could maybe get rid of these demons I'm carrying around inside me.'

'Any time,' Liberty said. 'Just ask away.' They rode on in the moon-whitened darkness, kept company by the sound of their horses' hoofs on the hardened dirt, the creaking of saddle leather, and the occasional yipyipping of a distant coyote.

20

Dawn was still two hours off when they crested Mimbres Hill. Giving their horses a blow, they looked down the long slope that ended at the moonlit desert a short distance from the ranch where Raven had been born.

At the time of her birth the Bjorkman cabin had stood alone in the vast unspoiled desert; now, the new owners had replaced the cabin with a big two-story ranch house surrounded by corrals and outer buildings, all of which were fenced in. Once it had been the only ranch in the area, but as more and more easterners arrived by train and wagon other spreads began springing up between the Bjorkmans' and Santa Rosa.

'If it'd been up to Momma,' Raven said as they rode down the slope, 'we never would've lived way out here. She told me that when they first arrived, she wanted to live in town. But Pa hated to be crowded and kicked up such a fuss, Momma finally gave in and they bought land here.'

Latt said: 'How come when he died, she — '

'Pa didn't *die*,' Raven said angrily. 'I keep telling you that he was shot by Slade Stadtlander!'

'I'm sorry,' Latt said. 'When he was shot, why didn't you and your ma move into town?'

Raven shrugged. 'Momma never said — though I always suspected it was on account of her not wanting to leave the place where she and Pa had had such happy times. 'Course, after he was killed and she'd been seeing Gabe for a spell, Momma sold everything and we moved to Old Calico in the California gold country to be with her step-brother, Uncle Reece — '

'That's where Ingrid died, isn't it?' put in Liberty.

'Yes, from typhoid fever.' Raven

paused, still unable to think of her mother without getting choked up, then took a deep breath to calm her emotions before continuing. 'Uncle Reece wanted to bury her there, but Momma made Gabe promise he'd bring her body back here and bury her next to Pa. Which he done. Only trouble was, by then the new owner, Lylo Wills, had built a barn over where Pa was buried. He denied it at first, but Gabe finally forced him to admit how he'd dug up Pa's coffin and reburied it in the desert outside his property. So, that's where we buried Momma, right next to him.' She pointed to a spot near the west fence where grave markers poked out of some rocks. 'Few years ago I bought that little strip of land just so in future folks couldn't dig up my folks' graves or build over them.'

* * *

Despite Raven's occasional visits, the two graves were overgrown with desert scrub and windblown sand. While the Dunn brothers sat and hand-rolled a smoke, Liberty and Latt helped Raven pull up the scrub and scoop away the sand and then they collected handfuls of Ocotillo and Spanish Broom that were flowering along the banks of a dry creek nearby. They placed the bright orange and yellow blooms on top of the rocks fronting the grave markers; then Liberty and Latt sat with the Dunns, so Raven could be alone with her thoughts.

When she rejoined them later, she wasn't crying but tears had dried on her cheeks and her expression told them how much she was hurting inside.

'Ready to leave?' Liberty asked her gently.

Raven nodded, swung up on her horse, and the five of them rode in the direction of Santa Rosa.

During the ride across the shadowy, moon-whitened scrubland Liberty explained that two years before she and Marshal Macahan had tracked three bank robbers into Indian Territory and finally caught up with them in Silver Rock Canyon. 'I want to warn all of you. The place is a stronghold. A few men with rifles could keep an army at bay.'

'So you never caught the robbers?' Raven said.

'Oh, we caught them all right, but only because the McClorys threw in with us.'

'Why the hell did they do that?' Bill asked. 'Most of the McClorys are wanted by the law themselves.'

'Exactly,' Liberty said. 'That's why they didn't want any outsiders bringing even more heat down on them.'

'So what'd they do — shoot 'em?' Raven asked.

Liberty shook her head. 'Some of the clan climbed up on the ridge and started a landslide that buried the robbers under a mountain of rock. Hell, Marshal Macahan and I never even had to fire a shot. Reason I'm telling you all this,' she continued, 'is so that none of you argue with me when I say that unless you're invited, the only way to

159

get into Silver Rock Canyon without being killed is from the south.'

'The south?' Latt said, surprised. 'You can't ride in from the south. You'd have to cross the Devil's Anvil and that's — '

' — the worst stretch of desert this side of the Sahara, I know,' said Liberty. 'But the south end is the only part of the canyon that isn't guarded.'

'Doesn't need to be,' Bee said. 'Everyone knows you can't cross the Devil's Anvil. Hell's fire, not even the Apaches or Comanches dare try it.'

'He's right,' began Bill. 'I — '

Liberty cut him off. 'My father crossed it,' she said.

'Drifter? When?'

'Years ago. He and Gabriel Moonlight both.'

'I never knew that,' Latt said. 'Did you, Raven?'

'I heard tell of it,' she said, 'but I figured it was whiskey talking.'

'Drunk or sober, you ever known Drifter to lie?' Liberty said.

'Can't say that I have.'

'All right then,' Liberty continued, 'we all agree it can be done.'

Bee Dunn said grimly: 'No offense, Deputy, but you ain't your pa.'

'Not trying to be. I'm just saying that Drifter and Gabe proved it was possible, and that's good enough for me. If any of you want to back out,' she added, 'I'll understand.'

'Not me,' Latt said.

'Me, neither,' said Raven.

'Nor us,' Bill said. 'We ain't quittin' for no reason.'

'Good enough. Then it's settled,' Liberty said. 'Now, let's get some rest. We've got hard times ahead of us.'

'It'll be worth it,' Latt said. 'If we bring in Roy and Quincy, dead or alive, it'll send a message to every outlaw in the territory.'

'Let's hope it's a message they can't ignore,' Liberty said.

'They won't be able to,' Raven said grimly. 'Not if it's served with hot lead.'

21

Thunderheads darkened the early morning sky when Liberty and the others reached Santa Rosa. As the five of them crossed the railroad tracks and entered the hot dusty town, the stench from the stockyards made them wrinkle their noses. They rode past all the holding pens, the cattle shifting restlessly as wind-blown dust devils swirled around them, and turned up Front Street.

The dirt street was rutted by wagon and stagecoach wheels and lined on both sides with boardwalks that fronted stores, cantinas, hotels, livery stables, a dentist, barbershop, and the sheriff's office.

As they rode between the oncoming riders, buckboards, and freight wagons, some of the pedestrians smiled or waved at Raven. She waved back, her emotions mixed between happy childhood memories and the sadness she felt whenever she recalled the sudden, wrongful shooting of her father as he and her mother were coming out of Melvin's Haberdashery.

Equally traumatic — and frustrating — was the fact that the shooter, Slade Stadtlander, had never been punished for it. His father saw to that. As the most powerful rancher in all of New Mexico, he'd hired the best lawyer in Deming, who persuaded the jury to believe that since Slade had been accompanied by the Iverson brothers, who were also drunkenly firing off their guns, no one could prove which gun had fired the actual bullet that killed Swen Bjorkman. Case dismissed!

'Raven — Raven, I'm talking to you.'

Latt's voice jolted Raven back to reality. 'W-What?' she said.

'We're here. Get down.'

Realizing they were outside the livery, Raven dismounted and led her horse into the stable, followed by Liberty, Latt, and the Dunns.

Inside, the owner, a weathered old

Swede named Lars Gustafson, greeted Raven with a warm hug and scolded her for staying away so long. She laughingly apologized, explaining that she'd been off looking for wild mustangs to sell to the army. She then introduced Lars to everyone and after leaving their horses to be fed, they crossed the street to the general store where Liberty bought two boxes of ammunition. She also bought five extra canteens, one for each of them, explaining that they'd need additional water in order to cross the Devil's Anvil.

Worried about their safety, the storekeeper begged them not to try to cross 'Satan's Desert' as they were sure to perish. Liberty thanked him for his concern, and rather than argue agreed to find another trail to Silver Rock Canyon and then led Latt and Raven out of the store.

Hungry, they walked past the Carlisle Hotel and entered the Rosarita Cantina to eat breakfast. No one felt much like talking, and after they were done eating they had the waiter fill all the canteens with fresh water before leaving the dining room.

Outside it was already hot. They crossed the street, collected their horses from the livery stable and headed southeast toward the badlands — a vast, hot, barren area made up of arid flatlands, rocky canyons, and ugly sun-burned hills that bordered the Seminole Nation and were a known haven for outlaws and renegades, whites and Indians alike. Liberty had never approached the badlands or Silver Rock Canyon from the south, but she knew the way almost by heart, having often listened to her father describe his and Gabriel Moonlight's journey across the Devil's Anvil.

They rode at an easy lope, not once seeing signs of human life. In fact any kind of life was rare. A few buzzards circled lazily in the sky, looking for carrion, and occasionally a coyote with a rabbit clamped between its jaws darted across the trail ahead of them. Otherwise, the sun-scorched landscape was desolate and, except for ants, devoid of living creatures.

Mile after mile, they continued to ride slowly toward the southeast. The sun relentlessly blazed down on them. Rocky outcrops offered the only shade and each time they stopped beside one for a few minutes to rest, the sip of water they allowed themselves did little to quench their thirst. The horses were just as thirsty and eagerly drank the palmful of water that was given to them every stop.

Eventually, dusk approached. By then the five of them felt drained and could barely find the energy to even talk. Exhaustion made them light-headed and woozy. Their lips were cracked and sunburned and their throats were so parched, swallowing was painfully difficult. Though no one said anything, all of them knew they were dehydrated and dangerously close to dying.

Evening breezes slowly cooled the air, bringing them some relief. Bats appeared in the twilight, swooping about overhead as they feasted on insects. Four of the five canteens were now empty. Liberty, worried that they might run out of water during the heat of the day and knowing they still had a long stretch of the Devil's Anvil ahead of them before reaching Silver Rock Canyon, insisted they rest until dark and cross the arid wasteland at night.

Dismounting by a towering rock that the endless winds had shaped into a fist, they gave their exhausted horses a handful of oats along with their ration of water. They then dampened their neckerchiefs and wiped away the salt and saliva that was caked about each horse's mouth. Then removing the saddles, they flopped down on the still-warm dirt, backs against the rock, and slowly chewed on strips of beef jerky and hardtack. With no water to spare to soften the hardtack, they broke the biscuits into small pieces and let each piece soften in their mouths before chewing and swallowing it.

Night fell. With it came a chilling wind that awoke them from their dozing. Rested and somewhat refreshed, they saddled up and rode east for a few more miles until they came to some low rolling sand dunes. Here, they turned north and headed for a range of jagged hills whose silhouettes made up the distant horizon.

Beyond the hills, according to Liberty, lay Silver Rock Canyon.

22

They rode all night in silence, pausing occasionally only to give their weary horses a blow, and, as planned, reached the southern part of the box canyon just before dawn. It looked exactly like Drifter had described it — a steep, dauntingly rugged, towering wall of rock that formed the closed end of the wedge-shaped canyon.

'My God,' Latt said as they dismounted and hobbled their horses, 'I can now see why the McClorys don't bother to post lookouts. Hell, even if you're lucky enough to make it across the Devil's Anvil, as we did, you'd need to be part mountain goat to climb up there.'

'Let me go first,' Raven said to Liberty.

'Why you?'

''Cause I'm used to climbing rocks.

Been doing it since I was no higher than Pa's stirrup.'

'Don't tell me,' Latt teased. 'The Mescaleros taught you?'

'They didn't have to, smart-ass. I learned by keepin' up with Apache boys my own age. Mother Nature never made a rock or a cliff they couldn't climb.' To Liberty she added: 'If you give me your rope, I'll help pull you up past the steeper places.'

Liberty looked into Raven's dark eyes and could find no fear.

'Go ahead.' She untied her lariat from her saddle and tossed it to Raven. 'We'll follow as close as we can.'

★   ★   ★

It was a grueling, dangerous climb. Not only was it steep but the ground between the rocks was covered with loose shale that kept slithering away, making each step treacherous and causing even the sure-footed Raven to occasionally lose her grip.

170

Liberty, Latt and the Dunns were not used to climbing and soon felt the muscles in their legs burning and cramping. But they grittily kept at it, now and then helping their weary legs by pulling themselves upward by the dangling rope that Raven kept looping around various rocks above them.

They had to rest twice before finally reaching the top and by then the sun had risen and they could see the entire canyon stretched out below them.

Lying on her belly, Liberty looked down and realized the McClorys were not just hiding out there . . . they were mining in the cliffs. She guessed they were digging for silver, since ancient legends about great silver deposits had given the canyon its name. Several mine entrances had been blasted out of the lower cliffs, each with a long wooden sluice sloping down from it. Crude planks steps descended from the entrances to the rock-strewn floor of the canyon, which was home to four rundown shacks. In back of the shacks were two outhouses. Not far away stood a barn with a shed behind it, and behind the shed was a platform supporting a large wooden water tank. Chickens scratched for grubs outside a nearby hog pen, while a rooster crowed atop the fence of a nearby corral containing several sleepy horses.

There was no sign of the McClorys.

From her viewpoint, Liberty could see the two lookouts posted atop the cliffs on either side of the canyon entrance. Both men had their backs to her, and telling Latt, Raven, and the Dunns to follow, she led them down the rocky slope toward the shacks. Though it was not as steep and there was less loose shale on this side, it was still a difficult descent. The five of them slowly made their way down between the rocks, trying not to dislodge any of the shale or stones underfoot. It took a while and twice they had to stop and take cover when a loosened stone rolled tumbling down the slope. But though the noise it made sounded deafening to them, it wasn't heard by the lookouts and finally they reached the bottom without arousing anyone.

There, as they crouched in the shadows behind the barn, Liberty laid out her plan. 'I don't know exactly how many McClorys there are,' she said, 'but I'm sure we're outnumbered at least two to one, so we need to jump them while they're still asleep.'

'Why don't we burn 'em out?' Raven suggested. 'Then shoot them as they come bustin' out, one by one. We mightn't get all of them, but we sure as hell will help even the odds.'

Liberty shook her head. 'We're here to arrest Roy McClory and Sam Quincy,' she said firmly, 'not gun them down. That clear?'

'And just how we going to do that?' said Raven. 'Knock on the door and ask them to surrender?'

'She's got a point and a point worth makin',' Bill said before Liberty could reply. 'If I knew there was a rope awaitin' me, I'd keep it waitin' and wouldn't give up without a fight.'

'So would I,' Liberty agreed. 'But the law says I've got to give them a chance to surrender first. With or without you,' she added, seeing Raven's defiant look.

'We didn't come all this way to back out now,' Latt said.

'Neither did we,' put in Bee. 'So, what's your plan, Deputy?'

'My plan,' she said, pointing at the nearby shed, 'depends on what's in there. If it contains what I'm hoping it contains, then we should have no problem getting all the McClorys to surrender without a fight.'

Before anyone could ask her what she hoped to find in the shed, she'd motioned for them to follow her and moved off around the side of the barn.

On reaching the rear of the building, she looked around to make sure none of the McClorys were in sight and then quickly crossed the open strip of land that separated the barn from the shed. Pausing by the door, she waited for the others to join her. She then quietly slid back the bolt and opened the door. The shed had no windows and it was dark inside.

'Wait,' Bee whispered, 'I'll light a match — '

'No!' she hissed. 'No matches!' She entered the shed, paused until her eyes became accustomed to the darkness, and then looked about her. She saw what she'd hoped for and smiled. Then telling Latt and Raven to keep watch, she waved to the Dunns to join her.

'Holy Jesus,' Bee exclaimed when he saw the stack of wooden crates. 'Dynamite!'

'I figured there had to be some in here,' Liberty said. 'Those mine entrances weren't dug out by pick and shovel.'

'Smart thinkin',' Bill said, eyeing Liberty with new respect. Then to his brother: 'C'mon. Sooner we get this over with, sooner we get that reward money.' He and Bee started stuffing sticks of dynamite into their pockets.

Liberty did the same. Then grabbing a handful of fuses out of a box, she kept some for herself and gave the rest to Bill. 'You boys got matches?'

Bill and Bee nodded.

'Good. Now, remember — wait for my signal before you light any fuses.'

Again the Dunn brothers nodded.

'Just don't be waitin' too long,' Bill said. 'Them McClory boys ain't shy 'bout using their irons.'

Once their pockets were full, Liberty and the Dunns left the shed and rejoined Raven and Latt.

Raven grinned as she saw the dynamite. 'I underestimated you, Deputy. This beats smoking 'em out. Now we don't have to waste good ammo 'cause there won't be no one left to *come* runnin' out.'

'I'm hoping it won't get that far,' Liberty said. 'My guess is, once they realize we've got dynamite, they'll throw down their weapons and come marching out.'

'Wouldn't count on it,' Latt said.

'Me neither,' Bill said. 'From all I've heard 'bout the McClory family, they'll fight to the last man.'

'Then we'll just have to make sure we're the last ones standing,' Liberty said. 'Don't worry. Only way you and your brother won't get the reward is if you're dead yourselves.'

'That'll never happen,' Bill said. 'Not so long as I got one stick left an' the strength to use it.'

'Just be sure to wait for my signal,' Liberty reminded. 'Like I said before, we're here to arrest these men, not blow everyone to kingdom come.'

23

The rooster perched on the corral fence started crowing again, its shrill cry echoing off the walls of the canyon.

Before the sound had faded Liberty and the Dunns had already taken cover behind some rocks facing the shacks, and Raven and Latt were quietly making their way toward the canyon entrance. Their instructions were to keep the lookouts atop the cliffs pinned down while Liberty and the Dunn brothers forced the McClorys to hand over Roy.

The rooster finally stopped crowing. As if it were a signal for the McClorys to get the day started, lamps were lit inside the four shacks, their light glowing in the windows. Within a few minutes, the doors opened and a dozen or more sleepy, yawning men — some half-dressed, others in flannel long johns — came stomping out. Neither Roy nor Quincy was among them. Right behind the men were several young men and teenage boys and two mongrels that ran barking at their heels.

All part of the McClory clan, they headed for the nearby water trough to wash up.

Before they reached the trough Liberty stood up and snapped off a shot. The bullet kicked up dirt in front of the group, startling everyone and freezing them in their tracks.

'All of you,' Liberty shouted, 'down on your bellies!'

No one moved.

'Who the Goddamn hell are you?' demanded Jason McClory. In his fifties, he was tall and bulky and had an unkempt dark beard that hung down over his bib overalls.

'Deputy US Marshal Lib — '

Her voice was drowned out by a gunshot. It came from the darkened doorway of one of the two outhouses. The bullet ricocheted off the rock in front of her, barely missing its target. Instantly, she hit the dirt. Beside her, the Dunn brothers opened fire, killing one man and wounding another.

The rest of the McClorys scattered and ran for cover. Those who were armed began shooting at Liberty and the Dunns, who quickly returned fire.

More shooting could be heard near the entrance to the canyon as Latt and Raven kept the two lookouts pinned down.

Behind the rocks Bill Dunn held up a stick of dynamite to Liberty, saying: 'How much longer you figurin' on waiting, Deputy?'

'See that water trough?' she pointed. 'Think you can throw it that far?'

'Reckon.'

'Then lob it over there, and try to land it on the dirt between the trough and that first shack. But don't get it too close to the shack. There could be children inside and I don't want their deaths on my conscience.'

Bill scraped a match on the rock and

held the flame to the fuse. It fizzled for a moment then went out. He flared a second match with the same result. 'Fuse must be damp,' he said, shouting to be heard above the gunfire. 'I'll try another one.'

'Don't bother,' she said as he reached in his pocket. 'They all came from the same box, which means they're probably all damp.' She and the Dunns ducked as a hail of bullets chipped away pieces of rock near their heads. 'Go ahead,' she said. 'Throw it anyway.'

'But — '

'That's an order,' she snapped. 'Now throw it, dammit!'

Bill shrugged and hurled the stick of dynamite toward the water trough. It landed on the ground, rolled a few feet and came to rest about ten paces from the shack.

Liberty rested her rifle on the rock, took careful aim and fired.

The dynamite exploded, the blast destroying the water trough and blowing a huge hole in the side of the shack.

Screams came from inside.

Liberty cupped her hands to her mouth and shouted: 'There's plenty more where that came from.'

Silence.

'Toss one over there,' Liberty said, indicating the outhouses.

Bill obeyed, the stick landing close to the outhouse from which the shots had come.

Liberty shot at it, missed, and fired again. The second round hit the dynamite, the explosion flattening both outhouses. A blackened figure staggered out, took a few steps and collapsed. Dead.

'You — McClorys — can you hear me?' Liberty yelled.

'We hear you,' Jason McClory replied from inside the second shack.

'Then throw your guns out and step out after them, hands held high.'

Silence.

Then suddenly rifles poked out the windows and doors of the four shacks, and everyone seemed to fire at once.

The roar was deafening.

Liberty and the Dunns ducked down, bullets ricocheting off the rocks above their heads.

'Told you they wouldn't go peaceable, like,' Bill grumbled.

'Throw one in front of that second shack,' Liberty said.

Bill obliged. Liberty fired at the stick. The explosion destroyed the front porch, causing the overhanging roof to come crashing down.

'Toss one over by the barn,' Liberty ordered. When Bill obeyed, she fired again, exploding the dynamite. The blast tore off the double doors and part of the front wall, and after a lot of creaking, the barn finally collapsed.

All shooting coming from the four shacks stopped.

'Hey, Marshal . . . Marshal Mercer?' a man called out from the nearest shack. 'This is Clem McClory.'

'What do you want?' Liberty asked.

'A truce . . . so we can talk.'

'Nothing to talk about,' she said. 'If

you and your family want to keep a roof over your heads, do as I told you: throw out your guns and come out after them. And do it now!'

No answer. But Liberty and the Dunns could hear voices arguing inside the shacks. Finally, Clem called out: 'All right, Marshal. You win. Hold your fire. We're coming out.'

Rifles and six-guns were tossed out of the doors. Next, men, women and children began filing out of each shack, all with their hands up.

Liberty waited until everyone was lined up before her then she and the Dunns stood up, rifles covering the McClorys.

'Where's Roy and Sam Quincy?' she demanded.

'Gone,' Clem said.

'Gone where?'

'Hell Town,' Jason said.

'Mean Violet Springs?'

He nodded and scratched his straggly beard. 'They rode over there late yesterday afternoon.'

'Don't trust 'em,' Bill said to Liberty. 'They's most likely hid somewheres 'round here.'

'You and Bee go check,' she told him, 'while I keep a bead on these misfits.' To Jason she added: 'Which one of you is Seth?'

'Me,' said a tall skinny youth with big dark eyes and bad teeth.

'Where's the girl you kidnapped?'

'What girl?'

'The one named Rainy.'

'I didn't kidnap no girl,' he protested, 'named Rainy or anythin' else.'

'Don't lie, dammit.'

'I ain't lyin', I tell you!'

'If anything's happened to her,' Liberty warned, 'I'll personally see that you're strung up for murder.'

'Marshal,' Jason broke in, 'Seth ain't lyin'. I swear it. He never kidnapped nobody. None of us did. Search the whole canyon if you want, and you'll see I'm tellin' you the truth.'

He sounded so sincere Liberty decided to wait until Latt was with her before pressing the issue. 'All of you,' she told the group. 'Get down on your bellies. Do it,' she insisted when no one moved. 'Pronto!'

She fired a round from her Winchester over their heads, making them flinch. Grumbling, they finally obeyed. Liberty kept them covered while she waited for the Dunns to return.

They weren't gone long. After checking inside the four shacks, the two outhouses, and the collapsed barn, Bill and Bee returned to Liberty's side, shaking their heads.

'If Roy or Quincy's here,' Bill said, 'they got to be hidin' up in the rocks someplace or maybe in one of them mines.'

'I told you they weren't here,' Jason said.

Liberty ignored him. 'While you were looking,' she said to Bill, 'did you happen to see a young girl — someone who looks a lot like Latt?'

'Uh-uh.'

'You sure? It's his sister and she's

186

supposed to be a prisoner here.'

'Well, we never seen her,' said Bee.

'See,' Jason called out to Liberty. 'I told you Seth never kidnapped no girl. Ever.'

'For now I'll take you at your word,' Liberty said. 'But if you're lying — any of you — about the girl or Quincy or Roy — I promise you, I'll come back with a posse. And next time we won't leave a building standing. We clear on that, Mr McClory?'

'Right clear, Marshal.'

'*Deputy* Marshal,' Liberty corrected. She beckoned to two young boys: 'You, and you. Pick up all the guns, take them over to that well by the barn, and dump them down it.'

The boys obeyed. Liberty waited until they'd returned, empty-handed, then turned back to Jason. 'Signal the lookouts. Tell them to throw down their guns.'

Rising, Jason walked toward the entrance to the canyon. The shooting between the lookouts and Latt and

Raven had stopped as soon as they heard the dynamite exploding, and now all four watched as Jason approached.

When he was within shouting distance, he yelled to the lookouts to throw down their guns. Reluctantly, they obeyed.

'Keep 'em covered,' Liberty shouted to Latt and Raven. 'Either one makes a wrong move, shoot them.'

Latt signaled to show he'd heard.

Liberty turned to Jason, who had returned beside her. 'We're going to borrow five of your horses, Mr McClory. Tell one of your men to go with us. Soon as we pick up our own horses, he can bring yours back here. Oh, and one last thing,' she added. 'If you send one of your boys into Hell Town to warn Roy and Quincy that we're coming, I'll burn this canyon down around your ears!'

Without waiting for him to respond, she signaled to the Dunn brothers to follow her and led them to the corral.

188

24

As soon as the five of them had safely ridden out of the canyon, Liberty dropped back a little and told Latt to ride beside her.

'You got some explaining to do,' she said harshly. 'So start talking.'

He guiltily lowered his eyes. 'I don't know where to begin.'

'Start by telling me why you lied about your sister being kidnapped.'

Latt hesitated, then shrugged and said: 'I knew you wouldn't take us along if I didn't have a good reason.'

'Dammit, even if that's true, why'd you want to go along in the first place? The McClorys mean nothing to you. So why risk your life — and Raven's — just to ride with me?'

Latt sighed and forced himself to say: 'Because I wanted to know more about you.'

'Why?'

''Cause . . . '

'I need a better reason than that.'

He swallowed, hard. 'I planned on killin' you.'

Shocked, Liberty reigned up. Latt did the same thing and for several moments they stared at each other in the broiling sun.

'Why in hell would you want to kill me?' she said finally. 'We've never even met before.'

'I know. But my mother killed herself on account of you, and I figured on making you pay for it.'

Liberty frowned, completely at a loss. 'Best run that by me again,' she said grimly, 'because so far you're not making any sense.'

'All right,' Latt said. 'But first tell the others to wait up, 'cause this may take a spell.'

Liberty cupped her hands about her mouth and shouted: 'Hold up, everyone. Find some shade. We'll catch up to you in a minute.' Turning back to Latt, she added: 'Go ahead. I'm listening.'

'Well, for starters,' Latt said, 'Latigo's my father, not my brother.'

'Why should I believe that after all your other lies?'

''Cause it's true.'

'All right, say it is. What about Rainy? Is she really your kid sister?'

'Yes.'

'But she was never kidnapped?'

'No. That part I made up.'

'What about Raven — why'd she go along with you?'

'I talked her into it. Said I had a good reason and I'd explain later.'

Liberty sighed and remained silent. She studied Latt's beautiful young face, his startling blue eyes, and decided he was telling the truth.

'How's all this tie in with your mother's death?'

'Momma adored my dad . . . would have done anything for him . . . even die if necessary. And when he told her that he didn't love her anymore, and planned on marrying you, she was so

191

torn up with grief that she couldn't face life without him.'

'So she killed herself?'

Latt nodded.

'How?'

'She swallowed some poison.'

Liberty closed her eyes, dismayed by the idea. 'I see.' Mind churning, she tried to digest this sudden ugly news. 'And you decided to blame me for it? Even though I was only a schoolgirl, and had no idea that your father was even married at the time?'

Latt shrugged. 'I didn't know that then.'

'I'm surprised you didn't shoot me on sight.'

'I wanted to. More than you'll ever know.'

'Then why didn't you?'

'On account of Raven.'

'She knew you planned to kill me?'

'No. Never.'

'Then?'

'She told me that she'd met you — that she liked you and your father,

Drifter, and that her mom did too, and . . . well, the way she talked about you, I realized you weren't anything like the woman I thought you were . . . and . . . the fact that I love Raven and hope one day to marry her made me wonder all the more about you. What type of person you really were, and . . . which is why I brought her along. I figured if she was right about you, she might help me to understand you better . . . ' His voice trailed off.

Liberty sucked breath in between her clenched teeth. It made a faint whistling sound, and filled her lungs with hot dry air.

'What about now?' she demanded. 'You still want to kill me?'

'No.'

'You're sure about that? Because if you're not, here's where we part company.'

'I'm sure,' Latt said firmly. 'I know now it wasn't your fault — that my mother probably would have done the same thing no matter what woman took my dad away from her.'

Liberty chewed on her lip, her mind going over everything Latt had said. 'Well,' she said after a long pause, 'I'm glad it never came down to gunplay.'

'Me, too,' Latt said. He offered her his hand. 'I'll understand if you say no, Deputy, but I'd sure like us to be friends.'

'I'd like that too,' Liberty said. She shook hands, adding: 'Oh, one last thing. Who else knows that Latigo was your father?'

'No one.'

'Not even Raven?'

'Uh-uh. Reckon I should tell her?'

'If you truly plan on asking her to marry you, yes. She might feel slighted if you don't. I know I would.'

Latt grinned. 'I'll do it. Thanks.'

'*Por nada*,' Liberty said. Together, they kicked up their horses and rode toward the others.

25

It was mid-morning when Liberty, Latt, Raven, and the Dunn brothers rode up to the gated barbed-wire fence that separated Violet Springs from the Seminole Nation. On the other side of the fence the hot, dusty little eyesore did not resemble its nickname: Hell Town. The streets were empty and quiet save for the snoring of two drunks sleeping against the side of the Bottom Dollar saloon, and the only things moving were a few stolen horses in the corral behind the livery stable and some crows fighting over the bullet-riddled carcass of a coyote decaying in the sun-baked dirt.

'Welcome to purgatory,' Bee said as he dismounted and opened the gate.

'If this is hell,' Raven grumbled, 'I wouldn't be caught dead in it.'

'The devil ain't particular where you

find him,' said Bill, 'just so's you find him.'

'Or he finds you,' his brother added.

'Oh, we'll find him,' Latt promised.

'Yeah,' agreed Raven. 'And we'll tame him, too.'

'We'll tame *both* of those weasels,' Liberty said. 'And after we tame them, I'm taking them back to Guthrie to face a rope. What's more, this time I'm not too particular *how* I take them — can be in irons or face-down over their saddles for all I care.'

Bill tongued his chew to his other cheek and nodded approvingly. 'Glad to see you're learnin', Deputy, 'cause learning's what it's all about.'

'Careful, Mr Dunn,' she said dryly. 'That sounded mighty close to a compliment.'

'Was meant as one,' he said, adding: 'I was wrong about you. You got enough of your daddy in you to maybe be a marshal after all.' Pulling his rifle from its scabbard, he levered in a round then waited for his younger brother to remount before nudging his horse forward.

Liberty kept quiet. She was pleased by Bill Dunn's compliment, but at the same time wondered if he was right. She sensed she was changing and not necessarily for the good.

Entering through the gate the five of them rode cautiously along Main Street, rifles at the ready, eyes taking in every doorway, alley, and rooftop as they made their way to the livery. As they drew level with the Bottom Dollar saloon, Liberty reigned up and eyed the half-dozen horses tied up outside. Not recognizing any of them, she stood up in her stirrups in order to look over the top of the batwing doors. Inside the saloon several customers stood drinking at the bar but all had their backs to her. She only needed a second look to know by their physiques that neither Roy McClory nor Sam Quincy was among them. Nor were they among the men playing poker at any of the tables. But she did see a familiar figure plodding up the stairs to the second floor. Disappointed, but satisfied her hunch had been right, Liberty settled back down in her saddle and rode after her companions.

The big double doors of the livery stable were open and the scrape of a shovel could be heard inside. Dismounting, the five of them stood there, looking around to make sure that no one threatening was closing in.

No one was. Satisfied they hadn't ridden into a trap, Liberty motioned for the Dunns to check behind the livery. She then told Raven to stay with the horses and to keep an eye out for Roy, Quincy, or any of the McClory clan that might be with them and then led Latt into the stables.

The hostler, a gaunt balding man whose sunken-cheeked face bore the scars of an old knife fight, was shoveling manure out of an empty stall. He turned as he heard Liberty and Latt approaching and on seeing her badge, immediately became wary.

'What can I do for you, Marshal?' he asked, leaning on the shovel.

Recognizing one of the two horses stalled to her left, Liberty said: 'For openers, you can tell me where the owner of that bay is.'

The hostler shrugged noncommittally. 'No idea,' he said gruffly. 'Fella just told me to grain him and walked out.'

'How long ago might that be?'

'This mornin', sometime. Don't rightly remember when exactly.'

'And the man with him, they left together?'

'Yep.'

Liberty turned to Latt. 'Fetch Raven.'

He hurried out and returned quickly with her.

'Stay here,' Liberty said, 'and make sure this man doesn't leave till we get back.'

'What if he don't want to stay?' Raven said as the hostler scowled.

'Shoot him,' Liberty said.

'*Shoot* him?'

'Yeah. In the foot or the leg, so he can't walk.'

The hostler backed away in alarm. 'You loco?' he said to Liberty. 'You can't go 'round shootin' folks for no reason, marshal or no marshal.'

'I agree,' she said. She smiled sweetly. 'So don't give me — or my deputy — a reason.' Nodding to Latt to follow, she turned and walked out.

26

Outside, Liberty found the Dunn brothers awaiting her. They shook their heads, indicating they hadn't found Roy or Quincy behind the stable.

'Follow me,' she ordered. They obeyed, falling in behind her and Latt, the four of them crossing the street to the Bottom Dollar. As they walked Bill explained that he and Bee had spoken to several townspeople, all of whom claimed they hadn't seen any of the McClorys for days.

'They're lying,' Liberty said. 'Roy and Quincy are here and I know exactly where the bastards are hiding.' She thumbed at the saloon.

'They wasn't there a few minutes ago,' Bee said, 'when we rode past. I looked.'

'Me, too,' said his older brother.

Latt started to agree with them, but

Liberty cut him off.

'You fellas weren't looking in the right place,' she said. Without explaining, she pushed in through the batwing doors, the others right on her heels.

Inside, Liberty ignored the unfriendly stares of the men drinking at the bar or playing poker at the tables and led Latt and the Dunns to the stairs leading up to the second-floor rooms.

'Wait here,' she told the brothers. 'Don't let anyone go up or down. And that includes the whores. Got it?'

The Dunns nodded. Winchesters in hand, they swept the room with their eyes. Not anxious to meet their stares, everyone quickly returned to what they'd been doing.

On the second floor Liberty stationed Latt at the head of the stairs. 'I'm going to check all the rooms. Anyone tries to make a run for it, gun him down.'

He frowned, surprised by her ruthlessness. 'What if he ain't armed?'

'Shoot him anyway. If you're not up to it,' she said, 'say so now.'

Her voice was as cold and hard as her narrowed brown eyes.

'I'm up to it,' Latt said. 'Just wanted to make sure I heard you right.'

'You heard me right.' Drawing her Colt, Liberty made sure it was fully loaded then went to the first door. She tried the doorknob. The door was locked. Banging on it, she said loudly: 'Open up!'

After a few moments a woman's voice said: 'Go 'way. I'm busy.'

'You got five seconds to open up,' Liberty warned. 'After that, I'll start shooting through the goddamn door!'

The lock turned. The door opened and a scantily clad young whore named Phoebe peered out. 'W-What d'you want, Marshal?'

Ignoring her question Liberty kicked the door open wide, pushed past Phoebe, and looked at the startled, naked man lying under the bedclothes. Seeing it wasn't Roy or Quincy, she turned and marched out.

As she stood for a moment in the

hallway, Latt looked questioningly at her from the head of the stairs.

She shook her head, indicating that neither man they were looking for was in the room, and went to the next door. She tried the doorknob. It turned. She opened the door and stepped inside.

The fat young whore cuddled against the man on the bed sat up in alarm, her eyes big watery-blue saucers as she saw Liberty enter the room.

Liberty recognized her instantly. 'Damn you, Ellie Rose,' she hissed. At the same time she recognized the man, who was reaching for the six-gun holstered in the gun-belt hanging over the bedpost.

He wasn't nearly fast enough.

In one smooth, blurred motion Liberty drew her Colt and fired before the man, Roy McClory, could even clear leather.

The bullet bored a neat hole in his temple, snapping his head sideways and slamming him against the wall. He slumped over, face-down, dead on the pillow.

Ellie Rose's wailing scream mingled

with the echoing gunshot as she cradled the corpse to her naked breast and desperately tried to revive him.

Liberty grabbed her by the hair and forced Ellie to look her. 'I should've listened to Bill Dunn,' she snarled. 'He warned me not to trust you!'

Her words were lost in the roar of a shotgun . . . as the closed door to an adjoining room was blasted off its hinges.

Liberty threw herself to the floor. From there, through the flying debris, she saw Sam Quincy standing on the other side of the shattered doorway with a smoking double-barrel shotgun.

She fired quickly, getting off two shots before he could fire again. Her bullets hit him in the chest, slamming him backward. He staggered and tried to keep his feet. It was hopeless. As he fell back, off-balance, and with the shotgun now pointed upward, he instinctively pulled the second trigger. The discharged buckshot blew off the top of the doorway.

Before the thunderous roar faded Quincy crumpled to the floor.

Latt now hurried into the room, both guns drawn, his expression full of concern for Liberty.

'You OK?' he asked her.

'Yeah. I'm fine.' Rising, she stepped over the carpet of splintered woodwork and stared down at Quincy. His eyes opened. He stared blankly at her. His lips moved but no sound came out.

Liberty coldly shot him between the eyes. He died instantly, head lolling sideways, eyes empty, mouth agape, a look of shock frozen on his lean, weathered face.

'You had no call to do that,' Latt chided. 'He might've lived to stand trial.'

'A bullet's cheaper than a hanging,' she said, 'as your daddy used to say.'

Her tone was so cold and heartless, Latt shivered.

'Seems to me, Deputy, you're gettin' more like him every day.'

''Cept I wear a badge,' she reminded him.

'A badge don't give you the right to kill.'

'Sure it does.'

'Not indiscriminately.'

'An escaped convict and an outlaw who just tried to kill me isn't exactly what I'd call 'indiscriminate.''

Then as Latt stared at her, tight-lipped and silent, she continued: 'Anyway, that's not the reason I shot them. I shot them because lately I've come to realize your daddy was right. For the most part, people are no damned good and the world's better off without them.' Before Latt could argue, she added: 'Help me get these bodies downstairs. I need to get 'em to the cemetery. Oh, and you,' she said to Ellie Rose. 'Get your fat sorry ass up off that bed. I'm taking you back to Guthrie.'

27

Raven, Latt, and the Dunn brothers accompanied Liberty and her prisoner to the train station in Clearwater. There the Dunns said goodbye to Liberty, again exacting a promise from her that she would notify the marshal's office that they were entitled to the reward.

Shortly after they'd ridden off, the train pulled in. Liberty purchased tickets for Latt and Raven to Santa Rosa, and a ticket for herself and Ellie Rose to Guthrie. The train wasn't full and the four of them were able to find seats together.

Once seated, Ellie begged Liberty to remove her wrist-irons.

Liberty refused. 'I gave you a chance to straighten out your life and you ignored it. Now you'll have plenty of time to think about your mistake behind bars.' Waiting until the train had pulled out of the station, she then turned to Latt and Raven, asking: 'What do you two plan on doing next? Get hitched?'

'He ain't officially asked me yet,' Raven said. 'And till he does, I'm not promisin' that I'll marry him.'

'Keep talkin' like that,' Latt warned her, 'and I may never ask you.'

'That'll be your loss,' Raven said. Then to Liberty: 'How come you ain't gotten married?'

Liberty grinned ruefully. 'I am married — to my job.'

'Lots of other lawmen are married outside their job.'

'I know. And maybe there'll come a day when I will be too. But right now that time hasn't come. 'Course,' she said, smiling, 'that could change if I ever ran into someone as handsome as Latt, here.'

Raven grinned as Latt looked embarrassed. 'He'd trade his looks for a few inches any day.'

'I'm warning you,' he said darkly,

'you keep it up and I swear I'll paddle the daylights of you.'

She chortled and winked at Liberty, who shook her head, amused.

Anxious to change the subject, Latt said: 'Deputy, you once said I could ask you questions about my dad.'

'Sure. Go ahead.'

'Did he really once shoot a man for callin' him Shorty?'

But the slip was out before he realized and Raven quickly picked up on it.

'Oh, so you're finally admittin' Latigo was your pa, not your brother? Well, 'least that's a step in the right direction.'

Latt looked at her in surprise. 'Y-You knew?'

'Sure.'

'How?'

'Gabe Moonlight told Momma and me once that Latigo had a son named Latham — '

'Dammit, why didn't tell me that before?'

'Didn't think it was any of my business.'

'Still could've told me.'

'Why? When a fella like you makes up a lie big as that, I figure you got to have a mighty good reason. Anyways, I knew you'd tell me sooner or later — you know, like, when you finally decided to grow up.'

'Damn,' Latt said. He shook his head in disbelief. 'If you ain't the most contrary girl I ever met, I don't know who is.' He rolled his eyes at Liberty. 'Deputy, what the hell am I goin' to do with her?'

Liberty chuckled. 'I'd buy her the biggest engagement ring you can afford.'

'Amen,' said Raven.

'As for your question,' Liberty continued. 'Yes. Much as I hate to admit it, from what I've heard your father did indeed shoot a man for calling him Shorty.'

Latt looked glum. 'Reckon it must be true, then.'

'Oh, it's true all right,' Raven said.

'Gabe Moonlight was with him. Said they were across the border in the *El Tecalote* in Palomas, and this fella, a gunslinger from Laredo, started bullyin' the Mexican who owned the cantina. Latigo told him to quit and, well, the man just laughed and called him Shorty. So Latigo shot him. Just like that. He was all set to kill the two men with him, too. But Gabe talked him out of it, and the men high-tailed it out of there like scared jackrabbits; jumped on their horses and rode off.'

'That's the story I've heard too,' Liberty said sadly.

''Fraid Latigo wasn't a man to poke fun at. Not if you wanted to stay alive.'

'Yet you loved him?' Latt said.

'More than I thought possible,' she admitted. She quickly looked out the window at the passing scenery so they wouldn't see the pain etched on her face.

But her reflection in the glass told Latt and Raven all they needed to know, and after exchanging understanding looks they dropped the subject and leaning their heads back let the rhythm of the train lull them to sleep.

★ ★ ★

As the train approached Santa Rosa, Latt and Raven stood up and Latt took their saddle-bags down from the overhead rack.

Liberty waited until the train was almost at the station then rose and shook hands with both of them. 'Thanks again for helping me — both of you. I couldn't have done it without you.'

'I'll never believe that,' Latt said. 'Not after seein' you use that gun.'

'Me neither,' said Raven. 'Hell, the way you handled yourself against the McClorys made me proud to be a woman.'

Liberty smiled, touched by their flattery. 'If it's all right, I'd like to keep in touch with you two. So if you'd let me hear from you now and then, maybe write a letter or send me a wire at the marshal's office in Guthrie saying where you've settled, I'll do my damnedest to come and visit you one day soon.'

'We'd love that,' Raven said. She paused and looked fondly at Latt before adding: 'Wouldn't we?'

He nodded. 'Maybe,' he said hesitantly, 'when Raven and me, you know, tie the knot, you'd come to the wedding?'

'Try to keep me away,' Liberty said. 'Hell, I might even drag my father along. After all, he knew your daddy well, Latt. And you and your momma too,' she added to Raven. 'So I'm sure he'd enjoy seeing how well you've both turned out.'

The train slowed down as it pulled into the station, causing all the passengers who were standing to grab the nearest seat in order to steady themselves. Then, with brakes hissing, the train stopped in front of the little yellow-and-brown stationhouse and Latt and Raven got off.

Liberty waved goodbye to them. As she did Latt's likeness to his father reminded her of other days, distant days that she'd spent with Latigo, loving him so much it had been difficult to think of anything else. Though she'd thought she had buried those memories deep enough so that they didn't hurt anymore, the tug on her heart told her differently.

She sighed, trying to fight down her emotions, and gazed out the window. She caught a glimpse of the couple as they walked off among the other passengers, many of whom were embracing their friends and relatives who'd come to meet them, and suddenly she realized how much she'd given up by becoming a lawman.

28

It was early morning, with the sun barely showing above the distant green hills, and Drifter felt a cool breeze brush his face as he closed the gate to a fenced meadow that was bright with spring wild flowers. A dozen or so pregnant mares were grazing on both the flowers and the tall, dew-soaked grass, and Drifter leaned his arms atop the fence, rested his dimpled chin on his forearms, and despite a lifetime among horses gazed in wonderment at the mares.

A tall, rangy, big-shouldered man with streaks of gray in his thick black hair, he'd just finished eating breakfast with the two Mexican hands who worked for him; and now, as he looked at the mares' swollen bellies, he wished that his daughter, Emily, was there with him so she could watch the foals being born. He missed her, more than he cared to admit, and constantly feared that as a lawman she might be in danger.

He was so deep in thought that he didn't hear the riders approaching. As they reached the ranch house behind him, his two mongrels ran barking to greet them.

Drifter turned to see who it was and since he was looking into the sun, for a moment didn't recognize them. Then, shading his eyes, he saw their faces. His heart jumped and, laughing softly to himself, he thrust his hands in the back pockets of his jeans and walked slowly toward them.

'Seems to me,' he drawled, 'a fella deserves to be warned ahead of time before you spring a surprise on him.'

'My words exactly,' Marshal Ezra Macahan growled as he swung down from his horse. 'At our age, hell, a shock like this could cause a heart attack.'

'Jumping Jesus,' the other rider said.

'To hear you two old range rats talk, a body would think you both had one foot in a coffin.'

'*Range rats?*' Macahan looked indignantly at Drifter. 'Did you hear that?'

'I heard, I heard.' Drifter scratched his stubbly chin. 'Seems to me, *amigo*, that certain folks around here don't have much respect for their elders.'

'Permission to bend her over my knee?' Macahan said.

'Granted,' said Drifter, adding: 'I'll even lend you a hand.'

'Get away from me, you two grizzlies,' Liberty said, backing away from her father and Macahan. 'Either one of you so much as lays a finger on me I swear I'll shoot it off.'

'Think she means it?' Macahan asked, straight-faced.

'I know she does,' said Drifter. 'She was wild growin' up and she got even wilder when you pinned that damn' badge on her shirt.'

'Should've known I'd live to regret it,' Macahan said wryly.

'I'm glad you both feel that way,' Liberty said. She pulled back her denim jacket to show she wasn't wearing any badge. ''Cause I turned it in to Marshal Thompson in Guthrie right before I caught the train here.'

Suddenly, both men lost their humor.

'Turned it in? What do you mean?' Drifter said.

'Just that,' Liberty said. 'I handed in my badge. I'm no longer a deputy US marshal.'

Drifter's jaw dropped. 'Did you know about this, Ezra?'

'Do I look like I knew? Hell, no, I didn't know.' Macahan turned to Liberty. 'If this is some kind of joke, Deputy, it ain't the least bit funny.'

'It's no joke,' she assured him. 'You can wire Marshal Thompson if you don't believe me. He was just as shocked as you.'

'But why'd you want to quit, for God's sake?'

'Because the job was turning me into someone I didn't like.'

Drifter frowned at her. 'I never figured you for a quitter.'

'I don't consider myself one,' Liberty said. 'Any more than I consider you a quitter for giving up being a wrangler to raise horses.'

'That ain't the same thing, Emily. I'm still involved with horses.'

'And I'll still be involved in the law.'

'How you goin' to manage that?' Macahan asked.

'By becoming a lawyer.' As both men looked shocked, she added: '*After* I help you, Daddy, see to it that all the foals are born healthy.'

Drifter looked at her, at his old friend, Ezra, and then at his daughter again.

'Be damned,' he said softly. 'Guess she truly means it.'

'Reckon so,' Macahan said.

Liberty looked at the big, tall, laconic marshal, who was staring at her as if still not totally convinced.

'Well, Uncle Ezra,' she said cheerfully,

'least you could do is wish me luck.'

He sighed heavily. 'That's all I ever wished you,' he said. 'Now get yourself over here, pronto.' He stretched out his long arms; she moved close and they hugged.

'Uncle Ezra,' he repeated happily. 'By God, girl, you ain't called me that longer than I can remember.'

'Better get used to it,' she said, stepping out of his arms. 'Just like you,' she added to Drifter, 'better get used to me calling you Dad.'

Drifter studied her for a long moment and then smiled. 'Reckon I can handle that, Daughter.' He gently kissed her on the forehead then wrapped his arms around her and held her close.

Marshal Ezra Macahan, a man tall enough to cast an even longer shadow than Drifter, watched them hugging for a moment, a smile creasing his leathery face.

Then as the morning breeze brought the smell of eggs and bacon and pan-fried potatoes to his nose, he turned and headed for the ranch house.

'You know something,' Liberty whispered to her father, 'this is going to be the best spring ever.'

We do hope that you have enjoyed reading this large print book.

Did you know that all of our titles are available for purchase?

We publish a wide range of high quality large print books including:
Romances, Mysteries, Classics
General Fiction
Non Fiction and Westerns

Special interest titles available in large print are:
The Little Oxford Dictionary
Music Book, Song Book
Hymn Book, Service Book

Also available from us courtesy of Oxford University Press:
Young Readers' Dictionary
(large print edition)
Young Readers' Thesaurus
(large print edition)

For further information or a free brochure, please contact us at:
Ulverscroft Large Print Books Ltd.,
The Green, Bradgate Road, Anstey,
Leicester, LE7 7FU, England.
Tel: (00 44) **0116 236 4325**
Fax: (00 44) **0116 234 0205**

SPARROW'S GUN

Abe Dancer

Before setting off in pursuit of his father's murderers, Will Sparrow must learn how to handle a gun . . . Miles away from home, he plans his reprisal while working as a stable-boy. But then Laurel Wale happens along, and Will discovers his intentions aren't quite as clear-cut as he thought . . . Meanwhile, his mother has settled down nearby with one of the territory's most important citizens. She wants nothing more than peace — but nothing is going to deter Will from his fateful objective.